the MERCHANT of DEATH

LISA HENRY · J.A. ROCK

Riptide Publishing
PO Box 6652
Hillsborough, NJ 08844
www.riptidepublishing.com

This is a work of fiction. Names, characters, places, and incidents are either the product of the authors' imagination or are used fictitiously. Any resemblance to actual persons living or dead, business establishments, events, or locales is entirely coincidental.

The Merchant of Death (Playing the Fool, #2)
Copyright © 2015 by Lisa Henry and J.A. Rock

Cover Art by L.C. Chase, lcchase.com/design.htm
Editor: Delphine Dryden
Layout: L.C. Chase, lcchase.com/design.htm

All rights reserved. No part of this book may be reproduced or transmitted in any form or by any means, electronic or mechanical, including photocopying, recording, or by any information storage and retrieval system without the written permission of the publisher, and where permitted by law. Reviewers may quote brief passages in a review. To request permission and all other inquiries, contact Riptide Publishing at the mailing address above, at Riptidepublishing.com, or at marketing@riptidepublishing.com.

ISBN: 978-1-62649-222-6

First edition
February, 2015

Also available in ebook:
ISBN: 978-1-62649-221-9

the MERCHANT of DEATH

LISA HENRY · J.A. ROCK

Tom Stafford,

If the winds of fate should ever blow you back toward this corner of the world, I hope that you will stay with me again. This time I'll be sure to warn you if Pastor Bob is intending to visit. I agree with you—I'm not sure that's where he ought to lay hands on the faithful.

—Denise from Dillsboro

TABLE OF CONTENTS

Chapter 1	1
Chapter 2	9
Chapter 3	19
Chapter 4	29
Chapter 5	43
Chapter 6	55
Chapter 7	65
Chapter 8	83
Chapter 9	101
Chapter 10	109
Chapter 11	119
Chapter 12	131
Chapter 13	145
Chapter 14	157
Chapter 15	169

CHAPTER ONE

Henry Page took the bus up 65 toward Zionsville. All around him, people stared ahead or out the window or at the floor. Never at each other. While Henry preferred cars—not always his own, and not always legally obtained—he liked the anonymity of public transport. All these people crowded together, heading in the same direction, and they spent most of the journey trying not to notice anyone else.

That was also one reason buses and subways were great places to pickpocket—so many people looking the other way. A crowd, but no witnesses.

Not that he was here to pick any pockets.

Unless...

He didn't know how long he'd be away from Indianapolis, or what he might have to do in Zionsville. And he didn't have any cash on hand.

He tried to remember what Mac had told him. *"You're a smart guy. I'll bet there are a lot of other things you could do to get by."*

Mac. Ryan McGuinness, FBI agent. The sort of guy who should have been on the top of Henry's Do Not Fuck With (In Any Sense of the Word) List, but since when had Henry played by the rules? Since never. Mac had actually gotten shot saving Henry's life. It was hard not to want the guy.

But Henry was needed elsewhere now, so he'd run out on Mac—for the third time. And practice really did make perfect, because this time he hadn't even needed to impersonate a police officer or clog a public toilet to get away. He wasn't sure he'd get another chance with Mac, but that was okay. He'd always known whatever flare of feeling had existed between them was temporary. *Too bad we never got to fuck.*

And they'd been so close too. Pants off, dinner abandoned, ready to roll.

There will be other inappropriate hookups. In places far from Indianapolis.

But at the moment he only wanted to hook up inappropriately with Mac.

The bus rolled to a stop in traffic just off the Zionsville exit. Henry drummed his thigh. He'd get out and walk if he had to.

He checked his phone. 7:35. Viola had been waiting twenty-eight minutes at this point. *If* she was still there. He ran through a list in his mind of possible ways she could have gotten away from St. Albinus, but it made him too sick to think about her wandering the streets alone. He'd have to get the story from her.

To her credit, Viola had picked an obscure location from which to phone him. Hadn't gone somewhere the St. Albinus staff would have taken her before on outings, somewhere they'd think to look.

What makes you think she's hiding from them?

"I need your help," Viola had said on the phone.

He got off the bus in the town center. The flag with a bulldog Viola had mentioned was a Hoosiers pennant over a café on Mason Street. A solid hour's walk from the care center. He ran all the way to the café.

When he arrived, Viola was sitting at a table outside despite the chill in the evening air. She had on jeans and a baggy, raspberry-colored T-shirt, and she was drinking hot chocolate.

"Vi," he said, keeping his voice hushed. However she'd gotten here, he had a feeling it wasn't with the care center's help or permission.

"Sebby!" She set the mug down so hard it rattled on the saucer, then she stood and threw her arms around him. They held each other for a while, Henry unwilling to let her go. Right then, he felt like Sebastian Hanes—a much younger Sebastian Hanes—and not like Henry Page at all. Henry Page had been on the verge of making a mistake with an FBI agent. Sebastian Hanes knew where he belonged.

Here, with Vi.

He took a step back. She looked okay. Her face, strikingly similar to his, had gotten a little thinner and more angular in the weeks since he'd last seen her. Her hair was lighter than his, and worn long, but they were the same height and still roughly the same build. She looked like a gaunter, less happy version of Henry.

And something had her *really* unhappy right now. Something had her scared. She sat back down. Henry pulled up a chair beside her and took her hand. "Vi, what's wrong? Why aren't you at St. Albinus?"

She glanced at him, then down at the table, shaking her head. "I can't stay there."

"Why not? How long ago did you leave? Do they know you're gone?" One question at a time. He took a breath. "Vi, why can't you stay there?"

She held his gaze this time, her eyes watery, wide, as though she hadn't slept in a while. "Something happened. Something bad."

"What happened?"

"There's an angel there," she said, in that soft, apologetic way she sometimes said things she was afraid he wouldn't believe. "A bad angel."

"A bad angel?"

Viola wiped under her eyes with her thumb. "Do you believe that, Sebby?"

"I think you should tell me what happened." He kept his tone gentle and squeezed her hand. "Did you see this angel?"

Viola nodded. She opened her mouth to talk, and then stopped. Got distracted by a waiter who approached. Who *stared*. Viola smiled at him.

Oh yeah, and there was that look. That one that was smitten at first, because of Viola's brilliant smile, but then slowly changed into something else. Something confused, and then pitying, the longer he stared. Henry could see the exact moment it happened. The exact moment the waiter saw that there was something *wrong* with Viola.

"A black coffee," Henry said. Then said it again to get the guy's attention. "Do you want another drink, Viola?"

"I want another marshmallow. I want a pink marshmallow this time."

"We don't have pink," the waiter said. "Just white."

"I want a pink one." Viola's voice rose, insistent.

The waiter looked between them. "We just have, um, white."

"Then bring a fucking white one," Henry snapped, and the guy scuttled away.

Viola's eyes widened in shock. "'Fuck' is a rude word."

"I know it is." Henry tried not to remember how she was the one who had taught it to him in the first place. "Sorry."

God, he was so fucking sorry. He'd been sorry for nine years now, because it was all his fault.

"Fuck, and shit, and dick, and—"

"Okay." Henry reached forward to take her hand before she could go through the entire list. "Tell me why you left St. Albinus, Vi. Tell me about the bad angel."

Her expression was very serious. "The angel took Mr. Crowley."

Henry let go of her hand and leaned back. "You mean Mr. Crowley died?"

Henry had been grateful these last few years for Viola's friendship with Mr. Crowley, an old man with mild schizophrenia who'd outlived most of his family. Vi and Mr. Crowley were in the same hall at the St. Albinus Care Center, where Viola had spent the last seven years. The bond between them had made Henry nervous at first. Mr. Crowley in midepisode could be frightening—and Henry would have thought his sudden changes in mood and behavior would be confusing to Vi. But he wasn't violent, and Vi seemed to understand and accept that her friend wasn't always himself. Or that he was always himself, but that self was complicated and sometimes difficult to be around.

To tell the truth, Henry was a little jealous of the friendship. Of the fact that Viola had someone else when it had always just been the two of them. Not that Henry begrudged her any friends she might make, especially now that he couldn't be around much.

You could.

He could worm his way into a high-paying job in the city. Stay in one place, make enough to cover his expenses and put the rest toward Viola's care. He wanted to be there for her, wanted to at least *try* to make up for what he'd done that had left her this way. But the guilt was thick and he couldn't breathe around it. It hit him the same way every time, knocking him back, away from Viola.

Cowards die many times before their deaths; the valiant never taste of death but once. Of all the wonders that I yet have heard, it seems to me most strange that men should fear, seeing that death, a necessary end, will come when it will come.

Amazing to him, sometimes, that he still recalled so many Shakespeare quotes—and that he still heard them all in his mother's voice, low and rich and somehow big enough to fill their apartment even when she whispered. Viola had always loved *Julius Caesar* for the blood and betrayal. Henry had preferred *As You Like It*: disguises, bondage and freedom, gender fluidity, and a happy ending.

He looked at his sister and tried to picture the girl she'd been—laughing along with their mother as Henry strutted across the living room, pretending to be Rosalind. He and Viola had taken some ribbing in school for their names. Having a name like Sebastian hadn't won him many friends; "My mother really loves Shakespeare" as an explanation had won him even fewer. But he was charming enough—and Vi was kind, funny, and a good athlete—that by the time they got to high school, most people could overlook the name thing. And the fact that, unlike many siblings who attended their school, they didn't pretend not to know each other when they passed in the halls. They ate lunch together, waited for each other after school and walked to the bus.

But their sophomore year, their mother had gotten worse. It was Vi who first discovered that not only was the money gone, but their mother owed the landlord, her rehab clinic, the power company, Vi's orthodontist...

Henry would never pretend to think what he'd done was a good idea. At the time, it had seemed preferable to losing their home. Except he'd ended up losing something a lot more valuable.

A breeze sent dried-out fall leaves spiraling down the sidewalk. Across the street, a cheer went up from a sports bar.

"No." Viola shook her head. "The angel took him."

"I don't understand. Who's the angel?"

"I don't know."

The waiter brought the marshmallows in a small dish, along with Henry's coffee.

Viola smiled at him again. "Thank you." She plopped one marshmallow in her cup.

"Vi, you're not making too much sense right now."

"The angel took him!" When she looked up, that fear was in her eyes again. "The angel's bad. If I go back there, I'll get taken too!"

"Aw, Vi, no." Henry leaned forward again. "You're young and you're healthy. Mr. Crowley was your friend, but he was really old. It might have been his time."

Viola stared at him, not looking fearful now but betrayed. It suddenly hit Henry how condescending he sounded. Since when did he treat Viola like a child? She'd always been better in the role of comforter than he was—even after her injury. "It wasn't his time." Viola's voice was low. "Someone *hurt* him. Someone *killed* him."

"Okay. Okay, I'm sorry." Henry showed her his palms. "Do you have any idea who?"

"I don't want to go back there. I don't want to go!"

"All right. Shh. You don't have to go back, okay? Not until we get this sorted out." Henry wasn't sure how, exactly, this was going to get sorted out, but he could worry about that later. "When did you leave?"

She bit her thumbnail. "This morning. Nobody saw."

How the hell did you manage that?

Henry could have used the pointers.

"This morning? Vi, what did you do all day?" He felt sick again.

"I took a taxi to the library. It was nice in there."

God. Now all Henry could think about was the hours they'd spent in libraries as kids. Because libraries were warm and safe and free. Because escaping into books was better than going home. When their mom was good, she was great, but when she was on smack . . . Well, the good times were harder and harder to remember. And at the end there had been none at all.

"I read picture books," Viola said. "Then I went and had cake for dinner."

"Cake?" Henry smiled, and thought suddenly of Mac and his health kick, and the way his eyes narrowed when Henry said provocative things like *cake*, and *caffeine*, and *sugar*.

Viola ate a marshmallow. "A man talked to me."

Fuck. "Who was he?"

"His name was David. He bought me a drink, but I didn't like the taste of it. Then he went away."

Henry was relieved. God, it was bad enough when Viola went wandering from the care center—she'd done it before, a few times—

but the last thing he wanted was for her to hook up with some guy. Because there were some things she couldn't have, because of her condition. Some things they both couldn't have.

Once, she'd seen a woman in the street holding a baby, and she'd looked so suddenly, achingly wistful that he could have cried. Those moments, when a part of her remembered what she'd lost, were hellish. Because the realization was usually followed with an angry outburst, and with tears.

"Then I called you." Viola put her purse on the table. It was a small denim purse with a kitten on it. She opened it and pulled out a piece of paper. Henry's number. He always made sure he told her when he changed phones, but was never sure if she wrote it down or not.

"Then St. Albinus is going to be looking for you."

"Am I in trouble?"

"No. It's okay. You called me. You did the right thing." Henry sipped his coffee. "What if . . . what if I go to St. Albinus and make sure the angel's gone?" He didn't even know what he was promising, not really. He didn't know how to vanquish imaginary monsters. Maybe by shining a flashlight under the bed the way Viola had done for him when they were kids. Or by putting on their mom's shoes and stomping around, because monsters hated stomping. For as long as he could remember, she had been full of fierce protectiveness and courage.

"Hold my hand and stomp, Sebby!"

Stomping and yelling had made the monsters go away. It had made the neighbors pretty angry though. And their mom. It was the sort of memory Henry felt he should have been able to laugh at, now that twenty years had passed over it. But he couldn't. He didn't have a single memory of his childhood that wasn't tainted by what had happened to Viola. By what he'd done.

Viola nodded, eyes huge. "I think I could go back if the angel was gone."

Henry swallowed. "I'll go there and try to figure out what's going on. But first, I'm gonna take you somewhere safe."

Safe was a relative term. He was going to take her to the only place he knew no one would find her. The only place Henry himself had felt remotely safe in years. It wasn't an ideal location, especially for Viola. But it was all Henry could offer.

He'd take her to the Court of Miracles.

CHAPTER **TWO**

Ryan McGuinness walked into the Indianapolis field office of the FBI wearing his usual frown and feeling as though he had more reasons than usual for wearing it. Not just because he'd recently been shot and was still trying to figure out a way of moving without pain. And not just because he'd had quinoa for breakfast, which wasn't the culinary experience the girl at the health food shop had suggested it would be. No, that was shit Mac could have handled with his usual cranky equanimity. What really rankled today, what really hurt, was that Henry Page had run out on him.

Again.

And Mac had been dumb enough to think there was something there. That somehow he'd dug through enough layers of bullshit and found something real underneath. He wanted to believe that, wanted to think Henry had been genuinely sorry to leave, but how the hell could he? It wouldn't be the first time Henry had played him for a fool. Or even the second.

He'd stopped in at Henry's hotel before work. The hotel that Henry was charging to the FBI, thanks to his status as a witness. He'd expected it to be cleaned out, but Henry's stuff was still there. A bag, some clothes, and a dog-eared Pocket Shakespeare. A pair of glasses with a bent frame.

So maybe he hadn't lied. Maybe he was coming back. And maybe Mac should stop obsessing about how much he was hurt personally, and concentrate on how much losing his witness—again—would cost them when Dean Maxfield went to trial.

"Hi, Mac," Paula said when the elevator doors opened. She was doing something to the plant on her desk that involved a tiny pair of scissors and a spray bottle. "Is Henry with you?"

"No."

Her face fell. "He was going to help me feng shui my workstation."

"Two things." Mac tried not to grind his teeth. "First, feng shui is bullshit. Second, Henry doesn't work here."

Paula huffed and hugged her spray bottle to her chest.

Mac rubbed his forehead. "Sorry."

"That's okay," Paula said primly. "You just got shot, so it's understandable."

Mac held her gaze for a moment. No, it wasn't understandable, and he'd been a cranky son of a bitch long before he'd gotten shot. They were both thinking it. "If I see him, I'll tell him to come and see you."

She brightened, and Mac continued on to his office.

Valerie Kimura knocked a few minutes later and didn't wait for a response before coming in. "Where's Henry?"

Mac turned to her, wincing suddenly. He maybe should have taken another pain pill, but he hated how sluggish they made him. "Did he promise to feng shui your office too?"

"What are you talking about?"

Mac toyed with the idea of trying to keep Henry's absence a secret from Val and waiting to see if he came back before anyone found out he'd been gone. But he didn't keep secrets from Val. "I don't know where Henry is."

He was impressed by how little her expression changed. "Explain."

"I was with Henry last night," he started.

Now her expression did change, and he couldn't tell if she was disgusted or impressed. *Disguspressed*—Henry's word. And Mac shouldn't have felt regret, sharp and quick, at that memory. Shouldn't be *nostalgic* for the good times he'd spent in the company of a con man. Maybe Val was neither disgusted nor impressed. Maybe she was just pissed off.

Mac ought to have been pissed at himself too, because he'd come *this* close to sleeping with a witness. Eight years of an almost compulsive professionalism—give or take a time or two—plus a determination to go down, not as a nice guy, but as an efficient one. All of that had snapped after less than a week with Henry.

"Mac."

"I know." Mac drew a deep breath. "We didn't— It wasn't like that." *It should have been. It almost was.* "We were having dinner.

Henry got a call. Something that upset him a lot. He was asking where someone was, and he told them he'd be right there. He left."

"And you let him go?"

"He's not our prisoner."

"No, but he's got a history of disappearing. On your watch."

That wasn't anything more than a statement of fact, a mild reproof, maybe. But Mac felt it like a blow, as if he should lash back. "Who knows when Maxfield will go to trial? We can't keep him on the short leash until then." He forced his tone calmer. Val wasn't the problem here. *Henry* was. "He promised me he's coming back. I'm sure—I *believe*—he will be here for the trial."

"He'd damn well better be, or so help me, Mac, we'll have to charge him with everything."

Not that any of them had a clue what *everything* was. All they knew for sure was that Henry had stolen a car and impersonated a cop. And had run from the FBI. But Mac was pretty sure there was much more to his history than that. Stolen property, forgery, crooked card games, numerous aliases . . . he'd hinted without ever confessing. And he was clever enough that Mac didn't doubt he was capable of all of it.

But there was another side to Henry too. A little kid in grown-up clothing. He wasn't half as bad as he pretended to be.

"He'll be back," Mac said weakly.

Val's expression didn't soften. "You know full well you should have found out exactly where he was going and when he'll return."

"I know. He wasn't about to tell me, though."

Val's gaze traveled the mostly bare walls of Mac's office. "When he comes back— Mac, I'm serious. You *can't* carry on an affair with him."

Carry on an affair. It made Mac sound like some sleazy politician. Carrying on an affair with his campaign manager behind his wife's back. "I know." Mac refused to look at her.

"I needed to talk to Henry. See if he could fill in some blanks in his statement. I couldn't reach him at the hotel." There was something off about her tone, something a little strained. She stood beside his desk, and he wished she'd leave. Just wished he could fucking have some time alone to feel sorry for himself.

"I went by earlier. His stuff's there. I really don't think he's bailed on us. And if he has . . ." *Then I'll find him.* "Then at least we've got Jeff." Mac said the name with all the bitterness he could muster.

Jeff Cavill. Former analyst. He'd been working for Dean Maxfield, the mob boss the FBI had just arrested. He'd also tried to kill Mac. Jeff had been cooperative about coughing up names and details, in exchange for a greatly reduced sentence.

"Yeah." Val sighed. "I really can't deal with another headache right now."

"What's the first headache?"

"You haven't heard?"

"I just got here."

"Mac, Jimmy Rasnick's dead."

Well, Jesus Christ on stilts.

Now there was a piece of news Mac wasn't sure how to feel about. The memories came in a surge—the years he'd spent tracking Rasnick, the unmatchable high of the day Mac and Val had caught him. The eventual realization that Mac would always be linked to Rasnick— that he wouldn't be anyone of note if it wasn't for that bust.

Mac couldn't pretend to be sorry the guy was dead. Couldn't pretend to be ecstatic either. Someone like Rasnick shouldn't be wasting oxygen or public resources. Yet Mac would have liked him to live a long life, all of it in prison and miserable.

"Fuck. What happened?"

"They're saying he hanged himself."

"Who's saying?"

"The prison."

"And you're saying . . . ?"

"I have it on good authority that Rasnick had bruises on his arms when they found him. And the bruising on his neck was not consistent with the belt he allegedly used."

"You think he had help?"

"Rasnick was Catholic."

"Prison changes people."

"I'm not saying I think anyone should dig into it. I don't miss the guy. I just want you to be aware that what's being reported differs from the actual circumstances."

Mac snorted. "That's a first."

"Right." Val almost smiled.

"Well," Mac said after a while, "I guess whoever strung him up did the world a favor."

Because Jimmy Rasnick was a piece of shit, and if there was such a place as hell, Mac was sure Rasnick was rotting in it.

"Right," Val said again, but Mac knew that neither of them really believed it. Whatever had happened in that cell might have been justice for every person Rasnick had ever gotten hooked on the drugs he sold, for every accomplice Rasnick had considered disposable once a deal was done, but it still meant a murderer was free. "I'm going to get a coffee. Want one?"

"I'm good."

She closed the door after her.

Mac stared up at the framed newspaper article on his wall. Rasnick stared back down at him. Creepy to think of him dead. And not as satisfying as Mac would have thought. Not with all those ruined lives he'd left behind.

Somehow his death seemed to sour the memory of his arrest. Mac had won the battle with Rasnick; had held on to that victory and gloated over it. And now it was as if by dying, Rasnick had gotten the last laugh. Mac remembered so clearly the thrill of that win: he and Val and their team had finally pinned Rasnick to a house in Meridian-Kessler where he reportedly lived with his wife, Flora. But Jimmy hadn't come by for days. The AD had wanted to bring Flora in for questioning; Mac and Val thought that would send Rasnick running. Flora seemed timid—Jimmy's little shadow—but Mac had no doubt that if they questioned her, she'd shut up, lawyer up, and find a way to warn Jimmy.

In the end, Val had proposed the idea of *using* Flora. By drawing from phone conversations of Flora's they'd tapped, the team had put together a recording in which Flora sounded like she was in trouble. She'd actually been calling a financial hotline about her debt trouble, but she'd been panicked enough, and she'd said the right things: *"I'm in trouble"* and *"I'm scared"* and *"I don't want my husband to come home to this"*—which they'd edited to *"Come home."*

It had been a gamble, but like Mac had told Henry, bad guys did crazy shit for love. Or for a warped idea of love. They'd placed the "call" to Jimmy. And he'd come home.

Flora had been out when he arrived, so the team had been able to storm the house before Rasnick even realized he'd been duped. He'd tried to run out the back, but Mac had grabbed him. Rasnick had fought. Mac could still feel that frenzied determination as he held Rasnick—*Not gonna let you go this time, you fucker.*

And then he'd slammed Rasnick's head against the wall.

Left a dent.

In both the wall and Rasnick's head.

He wouldn't have given have given any more thought to "excessive use of force," except that Flora had started making noise a couple of months into Jimmy's prison sentence. "Police brutality," "abuse of power," that kind of shit. Someone must have told her to shut her mouth before *she* got arrested, and she'd quieted down.

He opened his email. His attention was caught by an item about halfway down the list. It was from Dom Wolman at the BCA. *Subject: Request: Sebastian Hanes.* Henry's juvenile record, routed to Mac's email at last.

Fucking Jeff.

Mac had told Henry he wasn't going to look at the record. That he'd be satisfied with whatever Henry chose to reveal about his past. At the time he'd said that, he hadn't actually had the record in his possession, but now . . . It was tempting to read the report now that he was face-to-face with it. Besides, he might be breaking his promise to Henry, but Henry had broken his promise to Mac to stick around.

Mac opened it.

He didn't know what he expected. Something more horrible than what he found, or something less horrible? Maybe he just wanted what Jeff would have been looking for: an address. A background. A family.

There was only one entry on the record: Sebastian Hanes, sixteen years old. Prostitution.

Mac wasn't surprised. Henry had admitted as much when they'd been sheltering at the cabin outside Altona. Admitted it only because he'd thought Mac already knew. After Mac had asked him when he'd realized he could make money from conning.

"When do you realize? Shit, I don't know. The first time you spin some fucking john a sob story about your poor, sick baby brother who hasn't eaten in days, and he's so hungry, mister . . . And they get so guilty

they suddenly don't want their cock sucked anymore, and they're shoving more money in your hands than you asked for in the first place."

Yeah. There were no surprises in the report, except for Mac's visceral reaction to it. He felt sick. Henry had been sixteen. Just a kid. And logically he knew that kids that age, and kids much younger, worked the streets every day. But now he was imagining every one of them with Henry's face.

Dom was nothing if not efficient. He'd attached the arresting officer's report as well. Mac didn't read that. Wasn't sure that he wanted to know which street corner Henry had been hanging around on, whose car he had climbed into. Wasn't sure he wanted to know the name and address of the asshole who'd paid a kid for sex. He felt a hot rage well up in his gut. The sort of rage that didn't need a fucking target, not if he wanted to keep his job.

He scrolled through the report looking for something else. Henry's next of kin.

Brenda Louise Hanes. An Indianapolis address at the time of Henry's arrest.

He entered the name in the database and tapped his fingers impatiently on the edge of the keyboard while he waited for a result.

Brenda Louise Hanes: deceased, a year later at a Kansas City address. Drug overdose.

There was nothing in the file that would help him locate Henry now.

Mac closed his eyes. What had Henry mentioned about his past? That his mom had been an actress. That she'd been the one who inspired his love for Shakespeare. And that, like Mac, he was from Altona.

He hadn't believed that. He still didn't, not really. But he picked up his desk phone and dialed anyway.

Three rings, and then: "Hello?"

"Mom, it's Ryan."

"Are you okay, honey?" His mom's voice rose. "Do you need us to come back to the city?"

"I'm fine." His parents had only just gone home after dropping everything to be there for him after he'd gotten shot. "Listen, can I ask you something?"

"Sure."

"This is kind of a long shot, but do you remember anyone called Brenda Hanes?"

"Brenda Hanes . . ." She exhaled slowly. "Gee, I'm not sure. Someone from town, do you mean?"

"Yeah." He twirled the phone cord. "She would have had a son, maybe about five or six years younger than me. Sebastian."

"Oh, you mean *Louise* Hanes," his mom said. "She worked at the market one summer. Oh, that's going back a ways now. Such a pretty girl. She didn't stay in town very long though. She had these gorgeous kids. Just beautiful. A boy and a girl. Twins."

"Twins," he said. Fuck. Of course.

Twins.

Shakespeare.

Henry on the phone the night before: *"Don't go anywhere, Vi."*

It all conspired to tickle something in Mac's memory that a quick Google search confirmed. *Twelfth Night*. Sebastian and Viola.

"They were such cute kids," his mom said. "I wonder whatever happened to them."

He stared at his computer screen. Sebastian Hanes. Sixteen. Prostitution. "Do you know where she moved to?"

"I'm not sure. I don't think anyone really knew her that well. Did you just call me to take a trip down memory lane?"

"No!" He made a face when he realized how defensive he sounded. "I wanted to thank you for coming to look after me."

"Uh-huh," his mom said. "You're just like your father. You can't stand it when people make a fuss. But too bad. If my baby gets shot, you can bet I'll be there being embarrassing and mom-like."

"Summer camp all over again."

"That was one time, and you forgot your underwear."

"You didn't need to come running through the camp waving it around like a flag. I was fourteen. Do you have any idea how mortifying that is when you're fourteen?"

"Oh, please. What else were the girls and I gonna have to laugh about at book club?"

"I knew you did it on purpose."

"Is this line recorded? Because I'll deny it otherwise."

"Yeah, it's recorded." Mac smiled.

"Damn." She hesitated. "Honey?"

"Yeah?"

"Don't you ever get shot again, okay?" Her voice wavered somewhere between laughter and despair, as though it had started out as a joke but she'd lost her way somewhere in the delivery.

His heart clenched. "I'll try not to, Mom."

"And you shouldn't be back at work already," she said. "You should be on leave. You need to rest and recover. Come home for a while. It's been too long since you were in town."

"Ah."

"What?" Her tone was immediately suspicious.

"You and Dad haven't been to the cabin this week, have you?"

"No. Why would we? Why are you asking that?"

Shit.

"Um . . . It happened at the cabin. That's where I got shot. Sorry, I thought we'd already had this talk."

He distinctly remembered discussing this with his parents, right about the time the talking dog was in the room, and Shakespeare kept interrupting to ask if there was really spanking in *Kiss Me, Kate*, and how kinky it got. Mac had been on a shitload of morphine.

"You got shot in our *cabin*?"

"Well, outside." He winced, recalling the damage. "But it's cleared up now. I mean, as far as I know all the crime scene guys are done. And I'll replace the bedroom rug."

Shit shit shit.

"Why? What happened to the bedroom rug? *Ryan?*"

He rubbed his hand across his forehead and tried his very best to explain in a way that would not cause his mom to freak out entirely. Half an hour later, chalking that up to a failure, he finally disconnected the call and turned back to his computer.

This time he typed in a different name.

Viola Hanes.

He got an address in Zionsville.

CHAPTER THREE

A dog's low, rough bark made Viola jump beside Henry.

"Don't worry." Henry guided her around to the side of the house, to a scuffed white door. "That's just Doorbell."

He saw Viola look in the direction of the neighbor's yard, where a red and white pit bull stood behind chain-link. The dog lifted its head and barked again.

"Hey buddy," Henry said.

Doorbell kept barking, but he was wagging his tail.

"He always does that when someone new comes around."

"Can I pet him?" Viola started toward the fence.

"Maybe later, okay Vi? We should go inside."

The Court of Miracles was a basement apartment outside Indianapolis. Home to Stacy, Henry's friend and fellow con artist. Stacy had been in the game a lot longer than Henry had. She was fifty-six but had the energy of a woman half that age. There was a whole gang that hung out at Stacy's: cardsharps and con artists, hackers and forgers. They'd dubbed the apartment the Court of Miracles last year in homage to the gypsy lair in *The Hunchback of Notre Dame*. People came and went, and they all had their own projects they were working on, but it was nice to have a central location. Crime was a lonely business, Stacy always said.

Henry was nervous about bringing Viola here. The Court was a strange place at the best of times, but with Remy using, and Carson taking advantage of Remy's desperation for money, and Gerald back in town...

He would definitely have to rely on Stacy to keep Vi safe.

There was the added problem that he didn't want Viola exposed to these people and their world. *Bad people*, he couldn't help thinking, even though he was one of them. Viola was an adult, but her injury had left her as impressionable as a child. Doctors had estimated her mental capacity to be around that of an eight-year-old. Henry wasn't so sure. He still saw flashes of the adult Vi. Those flashes had given him false hope: surely there was a way to unlock whatever part of her brain had been shuttered off. He'd thought if he could just get enough money together, he could get Vi out of St. Albinus and somewhere they could offer her state-of-the-art treatment.

It had taken him a long time to accept that Viola wasn't going to be fixed. That the best thing he could do was accept who she was now—still his sister, still beautiful and amazing and smart as hell. Still his best friend.

For so many years, they'd taken pride in the way they thought alike. In their shared interests and ability to read each other. And yet Henry had always valued their differences as well, the things that identified them as individuals. Viola scorned romantic comedies, while Henry steered clear of anything that didn't have a happy ending. Vi was athletic, while Henry preferred art. Copying images and signatures. Designing costumes. Mimicking people's body language.

They weren't the same person; never had been and never wanted to be. Yet their closeness was what he'd clung to when everything else was going to shit. He couldn't shake the guilt, the feeling that he was responsible not only for damaging Viola, but for severing the connection between the two of them.

She should hate him. But he'd robbed her even of the ability to understand what an asshole he was.

"Don't be nervous, Vi," Henry whispered as he shut the door behind them and led the way down the stairs to the basement. "Some of my friends are a little weird, but they're all right."

Viola giggled. "You have weird friends?"

He turned to her and grinned. "I do."

"So do I."

He thought about Mr. Crowley. Fair enough.

He opened the door at the bottom of the stairs and led Viola into the Court. It was surprisingly clean. Mismatched furniture, a dartboard on the wall with an FBI recruiting poster taped over it—the poster was new—and a couple of Gerald's impressive art forgeries on the other walls. *"Paintings,"* Gerald insisted. *"They're only forgeries if you try to sell them as the real thing."* Which Gerald would do one day, no doubt.

Viola gazed around. "Is this where you live?"

Henry happened to glance down and saw that she was barefoot. He looked back toward the door. She'd slipped her shoes off when they'd come in.

Their mother had always tried to get them to take their shoes off before coming inside when they were kids. And ninety percent of the time they'd been too excited, too full of energy, too eager for the next stage in whatever game they were playing, to bother.

"This is where I stay sometimes."

Viola looked at him. "But where do you *live*?"

He hesitated. "I travel around a lot. You know that. I don't really live anywhere."

"I have to stay at St. Albinus." Viola didn't say it like an accusation, but Henry flinched all the same. "But not while the angel's there. Maybe now I could live somewhere else. Like here!" She hit his shoulder, then laughed.

He smiled and rubbed his shoulder. Didn't say anything about what a sad thought that was—Viola living here.

"About the angel," he said, leading her toward the kitchen. "Does Ms. Eiling think anything funny's going on?"

"Ms. Eiling doesn't work there anymore."

He stopped and turned to her. "What?" Barbara Eiling had been the director at St. Albinus since Viola had arrived there seven years ago. He'd met her once or twice. Liked her. Trusted her, which was rare.

"A man works there now. His name is Mr. Carlisle, and he shaves his face but forgets right here." Viola ran her index finger under her chin down to her throat.

"Why didn't anyone tell me?" A mostly rhetorical question. He didn't have an address, and it had been weeks since he'd visited St. Albinus. He'd called a couple of times to talk to Vi, but he hadn't made himself accessible to the care center for news updates.

Viola looked puzzled. "I don't know."

"How long has he worked there?"

"He came on a game day."

St. Albinus often had pizza parties in the common area on Hoosier game days. Henry knew fuck all about the football schedule though. "This month? Last month?"

"Two months. The first game day. He has a friend too."

"Who's his friend?"

"She's an old lady."

"A nurse?"

Viola nodded. Her attention had been caught by someone's shirt on the couch. Remy's. A couple of sizes too small for any adult, and ripped in strategic places.

"Well, what does Mr. Carlisle think of the angel, then?"

Viola didn't have time to answer, because Carson stepped out of one of the back rooms. Of course he'd be the first person they would meet.

"Carson," Henry said, not trying too hard to sound polite.

"Who's this?" Carson looked Viola up and down.

Fuck. Henry had been kidding himself if he'd thought Carson wouldn't be a problem. Just the glimpse of the guy's hairy gut poking out from under his shirt made him sick. Reminded him of too many men he'd known as a teenager who thought they had claim to anything they wanted. Who wore their lack of grooming like a badge of pride. Who stared at you, just like Carson was staring, because they knew it made you feel small.

He figured his disgust with Carson was fueled by what Carson had done—was maybe still doing—to Remy. Remy no longer seemed capable of refusing any chance to make a few bucks. And Carson had been taking full advantage of that. *"Look what this little faggot will do for twenty bucks,"* Carson had said incredulously when Henry had walked in on them a few months ago. And he'd tangled a hand in Remy's hair and pushed Remy's head farther down.

Remy hadn't stopped. Hadn't even made an effort to look at Henry.

"This is my sister," he said tersely. "You seen Stacy?"

"Taking a bath." Carson didn't take his gaze off Viola. "Your sister, huh? You two twins?"

Ya think?

"Yes," Viola said. But she stepped a little closer to Henry, and didn't make an effort to talk to Carson beyond that.

"Stacy?" Henry called.

"In a minute, hon," Stacy said from the back of the apartment.

The Court was pretty big—they had the entire basement of the house, and the couple who lived upstairs traveled a lot. Stacy got reduced rent for watering the plants.

"Who else is here?" he asked Carson.

Carson grunted. "Jo."

No Remy, then. Remy was out doing God knew what.

But at least he wasn't doing God knew what with Carson.

Henry glanced at the poster covering the dartboard. A picture of an agent in a dim room staring out a window, the words "FBI: Justice For All" underneath. Three darts through the agent's face. He wouldn't have thought anything of it a couple of weeks ago. Before Mac. You had to decide which side you were on. Criminals didn't work with feds.

Unless you fucked up, and they caught you. Unless they caught you and you were too much of a coward to tell them to go fuck themselves. Unless you made a deal—your fucking cooperation in exchange for their pathetic efforts to keep you safe from a psychotic mob boss.

Who kept you safe from the FBI? he wondered bitterly, thinking of Jeff Cavill.

And who the *fuck* had Mac been to tell him he could make something better of himself? To imagine Henry needed his advice on how to live his life?

Suddenly he wanted to throw darts at the poster.

He hadn't even been caught committing a crime; he'd been caught *witnessing* a crime, for Christ's sake. And he'd hung around like an idiot, and called the cops. You try to do a decent thing...

Stacy padded down the hall with a towel wrapped around her, leaving wet footprints on the blue carpet. Carson whistled.

"Oh, shut up." Stacy clouted the back of his head as she passed him. "Henry, is that really you?"

"The one and only." Henry hugged her.

"His name's Sebastian," Viola said.

Henry cleared his throat. "I actually have a different name with my friends, Vi. They call me Henry."

"Why?"

"Like the play."

Viola smiled suddenly. "Oh! Like King Henry."

"Yep."

"Hello, Viola," Stacy said, extending her hand. "Henry's told me a lot about you."

Viola shook Stacy's hand. "H'llo." She was studying the tattoo of some Eastern goddess on Stacy's upper right arm. Reached out to touch it.

Henry caught her wrist. "Um, Vi?"

Viola looked at him.

"It's all right." Stacy held her arm out. "Check it out. It's one of my favorites."

Viola traced the goddess's outline.

"Lakshmi," Stacy said. "Hindu goddess of money and good fortune."

"Oh." Viola paused with her finger on Lakshmi's crown.

Stacy glanced at Henry. *What's she doing here? What the hell are you thinking?* Stacy's face was never hard to read, unless she was playing cards.

He shifted. "Viola needs a safe place to stay for a while. Just for a little while!" he added, as Stacy opened her mouth. "Just until I can investigate something." He lowered his voice. "I can give you money."

Carson snorted. "You run a boarding house here, Stace?"

"Carson, could you give us a little privacy?" Stacy's voice was cool.

Carson scratched his belly and wandered back to his room.

"Is this a good idea?" Stacy demanded as soon as Carson was gone.

"It's my only idea." Henry heard Carson's door click shut.

Stacy turned to Vi. "Viola, I would *love* to have you stay here and get to know you better. But the house is a little full right now."

"I could camp outside." Viola glanced at Henry. "Like we used to."

He tried not to remember. "Gotta keep you inside, Vi. Make sure no one can find you." He looked at Stacy again. "Please? I swear, I'll be back in two days. Three max. Keep an eye on her. Don't let Carson bother her."

"I don't need a babysitter!" Viola said angrily, grabbing Henry's arm and squeezing.

"I know you don't. I know." He pried her fingers off. He tried not to let anxiety make him sound impatient. "But you need help with food. And you want company, right?"

Viola's eyes watered. She pressed the heels of her hands into them. "I want to see Mr. Crowley."

Shit. She was going to cry. And he felt awful, because for a second he was more concerned about her blowing her chance to be allowed to stay at the Court than he was about her distress. He could see Stacy warring between sympathy and the knowledge that it was completely impractical to host Viola here.

Just then, the door to the front bedroom opened, and Jo walked out wearing layer upon bustled layer of artfully tattered skirts, a black corset studded with tiny rhinestones, gray stockings with what looked like funnel clouds winding down each leg, and granny boots. Her black curly hair was done up in two long braids caged in silver, and she'd dusted her dark skin with some kind of shimmery powder.

"Henry!" she said. "I thought I heard your voice." She twirled, the layers of her skirts flying out. "What do you think?"

"Nice. What's the occasion?"

"Dream Con is coming up. I'm going to attend."

". . . Because you love nerdy trading card games?"

"Because I'm going to steal the country's most valuable collection of first edition Dream Wars cards."

"Ah." Henry stepped slightly in front of Viola, as though that might somehow shield her from Jo's casual admission. "Um, Viola, this is Jo. Jo, this is my sister, Viola. She'll be staying here for a few days." He glanced at Stacy, who closed her eyes briefly, but nodded.

Viola chewed her thumbnail, eyes still a bit red. But she stared at Jo's stockings and eventually smiled. "I like your socks."

"Thanks. They're not quite the right size, but I like them. I'm going as Admirella Cesan. I want the costume to be good, but not so good that I attract a lot of attention." She grinned. "And of course I went for the character who's a cat burglar."

Henry tried to laugh. "I don't really follow nerd culture." He wanted to get Jo off the subject of stealing. He'd never been *ashamed* of what he and the others did, exactly. He considered it a necessity, and there were a lot of times he enjoyed playing the system. But now it seemed all wrong. This place. The dartboard. The people. What they did. He wished he could have led Viola into some luxury apartment he'd bought with his own damn money and said, *Here. You can live here, and you never have to go back to a care center.*

He used to imagine that all the time—that one day he'd find a way to bring Viola home, to look after her himself. But it had never been possible. Any money he made had to go to St. Albinus—a top-notch care center, to be sure, but no substitute for a home. He was stuck. He couldn't stop paying for Viola to be there, but he couldn't afford to get her out if the bills kept sucking him dry.

Stacy nudged him. "You heard from Remy?"

Henry shook his head.

"He went off with Lonny a couple of days ago."

Shit. Lonny Harris used to be a half-decent fence. Now he didn't do much but shoot up. Lonny and Remy had bonded over a mutual love of heroin, and now whenever Lonny was in town, they ended up in each other's company.

"Not here." Henry kept his voice low. He nodded at Viola, who was still studying the pattern of Jo's stocking. Her fingers were twitching, like she was aching to touch.

"Just thought you should know."

Like Henry needed one more thing to worry about right now.

"Are you playing dress-up?" Viola asked Jo, looking up.

"You bet I am. I'll have to get you to model some costumes for me while you're here. Maybe some boy's outfits, since you're so tall."

Her words jolted Henry. He still didn't have a plan for how to investigate the bad angel. But now he wondered . . .

He was never going to get access to the St. Albinus facility as a visitor. And he'd already impersonated a doctor once this week—it would be pushing his luck to try that again. Plus he'd looked at the embroidery on his borrowed lab coat since then and seen that it said "Patricia Gordon, Makeup Artist" on it. So, you know, oops.

He also knew that as long as Viola was missing, St. Albinus would be looking for her. And as long as they were looking for her, she was in danger.

There was only one plan he could think of that would both give him inside access to the care center and end St. Albinus's search for Viola. He'd played a lot of roles in his life, but never one like this. But if Rosalind could manage it in *As You Like It*, if Portia could manage it in *The Merchant of Venice* . . .

"Jo," he said. "I'm gonna need you to help me with a costume."

"Sure." Jo straightened her skirt. "What do you need?"

"I need you to make me look like Viola."

Jo tilted her head. "You already look like her."

He took a deep breath. You didn't think about failure going into something like this. You couldn't afford to.

"I know," he said. "But Jo? I need you to make me look *exactly* like her."

CHAPTER FOUR

A file landed on Mac's desk with a thump.

He looked up at Val. "What's this?"

"A little welcome back gift from Indianapolis's finest," she said. "Homicide."

Mac opened the file. Saw the crime scene photographs of a shooting vic with a hole in his forehead. He was pretty sure he didn't know the face. He turned to the guy's name on the autopsy report, which shed no light on things at all. "So why is John Doe on my desk and not some cop's?"

"Because, look close at the chest."

He looked. Another hole, right through the guy's breast pocket.

"The head and the heart." Mac ignored the chill that settled in him. "Just the way Rasnick used to do it."

"Yep. You also received this." Val passed him a sheet of paper. On it was a photocopy of Rasnick's obit, and underneath, in cutout letters, "THIS IS ON YOU, PIG."

"Still getting mail from my secret admirer?" Mac asked. He'd received his share of threatening letters since putting Rasnick away.

"Seems like it."

"I'm not even a cop. Why are they calling me a pig?" He met Val's gaze. "You think there's a connection?"

"I don't know. Homicide shared John Doe with us. They think the murder might be a signal from one of Rasnick's former cohorts."

Mac closed the file. "I'll look into it."

"From your desk," Val said.

"What?"

"You'll look into it from your desk. You're injured, Mac. You probably shouldn't even be back at work. You're certainly not going out into the field."

"Yes, ma'am."

Val rolled her eyes and left him to it.

Mac went through John Doe's file again, then put it aside and checked his email. He found himself picking up the sticky note where he'd written Viola Hanes's Zionsville address and staring at that instead.

Finding Henry had to be his first priority, and heading out to Zionsville surely didn't count as fieldwork. It was more of a friendly visit.

Mac's attention was caught by the sudden hush that descended. He saw two men and a woman he didn't recognize out on the floor.

OPR. Office of Professional Responsibility.

Their reputation was enough to shut down conversations in midlaugh, but Mac didn't hate them—had no reason to. He'd always played by the rules. Sure, it was a pain in the ass when they investigated some bullshit complaint, but there was no point getting defensive about it. In light of the news Val had broken when he'd arrived at work, Mac half expected it to be about Jimmy Rasnick.

It wasn't.

"Mac." Val appeared in his doorway again. "Do you have a minute?"

"Sure." Mac stood up and slipped the sticky note into his pocket, then followed Val to the conference room. Sat down beside her.

The two men were studying files and didn't look at Mac. But the woman was staring at him. She had dark hair pulled into a ponytail at her nape and wore a navy suit. "Agent McGuinness?" she said. "Agent Janice Bixler, OPR. This is Agent Lawrence and Agent Talbot. We'd like to ask you a few questions."

"All right."

Agent Janice Bixler didn't ask him any questions, though. She left that to one of the guys—Lawrence or Talbot—and sat taking notes on her sleek black tablet while Mac went over, in painstaking detail, what exactly had happened at the cabin in Altona.

Well, not exactly. There was some stuff that Mac was keeping to himself. The impromptu Shakespeare performance. The stolen groceries. And especially the way Henry had just fucking melted against him when they'd kissed.

It was strange to have a name to put to the guy he'd killed. Robert Jones. And such a prosaic name. A schoolteacher name. A guy-in-the-street name. Not a hired-killer name.

For an hour and a half, Mac went through the sequence of events in the cabin. And didn't even get pissed when one of them asked him if he'd considered using an alternative to lethal force.

"He was a hit man. He was there to kill my witness."

His witness.

"The witness you then lost," the guy said.

Okay, Mac was keeping his cool, but he officially did not like this guy. He was even more creeped out by Janice Bixler, who sat making notes, her expression never changing. Every few minutes, though, Mac could feel her gaze on him. "After I got shot, yes, I lost him. He ran. Anyone would have."

"Your office seems to have some trouble holding on to this particular witness," the guy said. "Where is he now?"

Val bristled. "Mr. Page is staying nearby. If you need him brought in for questioning, that's certainly something that can be arranged, but I assure you that his version of events matches Agent McGuinness's. I took his statement myself."

Of all the things that Mac admired most about Val, it was her ability to bald-faced lie. He leaned back in his seat and let her take over.

"In addition, Agent McGuinness has my full support in this matter." Val closed her folder. "And I would advise him not to continue this interview until he is medically cleared to do so."

"We'll talk again soon," the guy said.

"Actually, I have one more question," Bixler said, looking up at Mac.

He waited. Nothing warm in her eyes. It was like staring into a hole in the ground.

"How well do you know your witness, Agent McGuinness?"

He couldn't speak for a moment. His mind was caught on an image of Henry, lying on Mac's bed, his pants around his ankles, his cock hard and straining his underwear.

"Not very well. We didn't know each other prior to the Maxfield case."

"But you had some time to get to know him at the cabin?" Janice was still staring at him.

He didn't understand the point of the question. There was no way OPR could know how Mac and Henry had spent their time in Altona.

"Mr. Page is a difficult man to get to know."

And wasn't that the truth?

Janice stood. "We'll be in touch."

They left.

"Those assholes." Val glowered at the door after them. "Did you see the size of that report? We would have been here all day."

Mac stretched carefully, mindful of pulling his stitches. "But I'm good, right? With the shooting?"

"Of course you are." Val put a hand over his and squeezed. "You're alive and a bad guy is dead. That's a good result. You know what OPR's like. It's easy in hindsight to pick apart a decision that you made in milliseconds. We've all been there, Mac. The worst thing you can do is start doubting your own judgment."

"I know that," he said, but knowing it and feeling it were two different things.

"Mac." Her voice was low. "I might have gotten a look at that report when Thing One was staring at my ass."

"Yeah?" Mac frowned.

"I saw Louie Gallo's name."

Louie Gallo.

Shit, that was going back a few years now. Louie Gallo had run an illegal fighting ring. Mac had taken the lead on the case. Louie, an ex-boxer, had fought like a cornered dog during his arrest. Bloodiest mug shot ever. The picture of Louie with his nose pushed halfway across his face had held pride of place in the field office meal room for weeks, until Paula had complained it put her off her lunch and it was taken down.

"Why the hell would OPR be interested in Louie Gallo?" he asked, and then groaned. "Shit. They're interested in me."

"Yeah, it seems that way."

"Why? Because of the shooting? Or because of something else?"

Louie Gallo. Jimmy Rasnick. Yeah, Mac occasionally took suspects down hard.

When it was necessary.

When they started it.

"I don't know." Val's face was drawn with concern. "Look, it's probably nothing. After Jeff, they're probably investigating all of us, right?"

"Sure," Mac said dryly. "And they're starting with me just because."

"Yeah."

Mac rubbed a hand across the gauze underneath his shirt. He didn't want to deal with this shit at the moment. What he wanted was to find Henry, remind him that he'd agreed to testify and couldn't just fuck off whenever he wanted.

And to find out what was going on with Henry. With Henry and him. If it was anything at all, or just another game. If those few times he'd looked into Henry's eyes and seen *something*, if those moments were real. If Henry was real.

Henry, Sebastian, or someone else entirely.

His chest ached, and he grimaced.

"Okay?" Val asked.

He sighed. "Val? Is it too late to put in for sick leave?"

Henry had four missed calls from St. Albinus by the time he arrived there. Viola had been missing for twenty-four hours, and they'd only made four attempts to call her next of kin. Barbara Eiling had run a tighter ship than that. Back when Viola had first been placed at St. Albinus, she'd run off several times, and each time someone had called Henry within the first twenty minutes. Sometimes he'd missed those calls; he'd been between towns or between phones—but they'd always called.

"Mr. Hanes," Barbara had told him after that first month, her voice arch with barely muted disapproval, *"perhaps if you wish to be a part of Viola's care, you should make more of an effort to be available to us."*

He'd felt as small and guilty as he had in first grade when his teacher had made him apologize in front of the whole class for taking Jason Hall's Transformer toy without asking.

This time the calls were from Dr. Seth Carlisle, who didn't sound disapproving so much as tired in the voice mail he left after his fourth attempt. "Mr. Hanes. Please give us a call at your earliest convenience. We need to speak to you regarding your sister. Consider it urgent."

He'd spent the night at the Court with Vi, then taken the bus to Zionsville this morning. Had walked from downtown to the outskirts, where the care center was tucked in a circle of trees like some cultish compound. He'd never really thought of it that way before. When he'd first seen the place, he'd thought it was beautiful. He'd *needed* it to be beautiful. Safe, friendly, and loving. He'd needed it to be the opposite of the state hospital where Viola had spent the first year after her injury. That place had been overbooked and understaffed, the nurses short-tempered, the doctors pessimistic. And by that time their mother had already checked out mentally, her mind drug addled, her body collapsing. Henry had felt painfully alone under the fluorescent lights in Viola's ward, faced with her confusion, the smallness of her bed, her pathetic congealed food, the machines she was routinely hooked to that studied her brain activity.

He'd tried to picture Viola's brain. Tried to imagine how brutal the impact must have been to jar it so badly that parts of it went off like a power cut. Tried to picture the injury, the textbook idea of it, while keeping at bay the memories of what exactly had happened. But that never worked. As soon as he pictured her brain, he was back in his room in their mother's house in Columbus, and two shadows were struggling.

"*Get* off *him!*" Viola had yelled, trying to haul J.J. away from Henry.

J.J. had grunted as Viola's fist connected; he turned and threw her off in one easy movement, the same way Henry slung his backpack from his shoulder onto the kitchen chair each day after school.

The room had been dark except for a soft spread of yellow light coming in through the half-open door. Henry hadn't been able to see where Viola had landed at first, and one of his legs was still tangled in the sheet. And J.J. hadn't done anything, even when Henry screamed at him to turn on the light. By the time Henry had found Viola's body, felt the wetness beneath it, J.J. was pulling on his pants. Henry had stopped yelling at him about the light, because he didn't want to see.

But J.J. had opened the door wide, and suddenly Henry was huddled in a stark spotlight with a tragedy of his doing.

911. The ambulance. All the while, their mother was passed out. And when she'd found out what had happened, when Henry had called her from the hospital and she was finally sober enough to answer, she hadn't even screamed or cried until she'd heard the increasing hysteria in Henry's voice. Until he'd infected her with it.

Over the next few months, she'd been just as unresponsive. If she was sober enough to visit the hospital, she stared at Viola like a kid eyeing a food she didn't want to eat. Or she brought things Viola didn't want or need—a pink plastic hairbrush, chicken nuggets, DVDs that couldn't be played, a necklace she'd worn in a production of *The Taming of the Shrew*.

Henry had started imagining sometimes during these hospital visits that he was in a scene in a play. And even though the writing and the situation were a bit hackneyed, he still had to give it his all as an actor, had to imbue tired words and clichéd gestures with new meaning. If he took Viola's hand, if he told her things would be all right, he was doing the same thing everyone who'd ever sat bedside at a hospital had done. But he *meant* it. He meant it when he said he'd help her, that he loved her. That he was sorry. He just didn't know what to do yet, and his own guilt tripped him up, kept him focused on himself. Giving, truly giving, his energy and resources to someone else would mean accepting that there were things beyond his control. That the past was irretrievable, and that he now had to focus on a present that was neither ideal nor fair.

Most things nowadays were within Henry's control. If he needed money, he got it. A new identity? Done. If he was falling for someone he shouldn't fall for, he bailed. It wasn't that fucking hard to make life your bitch.

As he approached the brick building, he ran a hand self-consciously through his synthetic hair. The wig Jo had given him was good—*"That's because it cost three hundred and fifty dollars. Do not let anything happen to it"*—and she'd styled it just like Vi's hair. She'd also given him a shave so close he'd been convinced she was taking off a couple of layers of skin as well. She'd done his makeup, shading the hollows of his cheeks so he looked a little thinner, reddening his mouth in the places where Viola chewed her lip. Then he and Vi had swapped clothes, and even Stacy had been impressed by the transformation. Jo had given him a bra with slight padding to wear under Viola's T-shirt, as well as a pair of women's underwear, and Viola had laughed at that.

The only tricky part had been the shoes. Henry's feet were bigger than Vi's, so he'd had to borrow a pair of purple sneakers from Jo that looked sort of like a pair Vi had. And even though Jo's size was closer to his, the shoes still pinched when he walked.

For a moment, he'd let himself get swept up in the fun of the disguise. On the bus, he'd been relieved and pleased when someone said, *"Excuse me, miss."*

Now he was nearly as anxious as he'd been showing up on Mac's doorstep the evening before. What was he thinking? Just because the cross-dressing thing worked for Shakespeare's characters didn't mean he could pull it off in real life.

He focused on the landscaping. Beautiful work. Pumpkins and vines in the mulch where the summer flowers had been. The front lawn was raked, and the maples had turned red. Before he could get close to the entrance, a woman came running out.

"Viola!" she exclaimed. "Viola, *where* have you been?"

Henry lost track of the "We've been worried sick"s and the "You know you can't go wandering off like that"s as he was led inside. He was actually pulling this off. This woman believed he was Vi.

"It's really not safe." The woman took Henry's hand. Viola'd had gloves in her jeans pockets, and it was cool enough out that he had felt he could get away with wearing them to hide that his hands were slightly larger, more masculine than Vi's. "And without a coat!" He caught a glimpse of the woman's name tag. Sarah Metzger. He didn't think he'd met her before on past visits. "Where did you go?"

"For a walk." He made his voice soft, high, like Viola's.

"You can walk on the grounds," Sarah said firmly. They went inside. The reception area was cheery—a sort of atrium with a round front desk. There were signs behind the desk with arrows pointing to the right for residents' rooms and left for staff offices. They turned right and went down a long, carpeted hall with doors on either side. Each door had a name tag designed by the resident, or sometimes the staff, if a resident couldn't or didn't want to do his or her own.

They passed one door where the name tag had been removed. All that was left was a sticky square where the tape had been.

"Now, I know you miss Mr. Crowley," Sarah said. She looked tired. "But you must stop wandering off. Dr. Carlisle was going to call the *police*!"

He should have, Henry thought. Weren't there procedures in place for this sort of thing? What the hell had happened to their duty of care?

"Sorry," he murmured.

"Okay." Sarah sighed. "Here we are. I'll go and tell everyone you're back."

Henry stepped into Vi's room.

It was a *good* room, but nothing could disguise the fact that this was a medical facility first and foremost. The bed had rails, and what looked like a television remote control hanging from the side so that Vi could make the bed go up or down. It was a reminder that most of the patients at St. Albinus were elderly or infirm. He'd only ever seen Vi adjust the bed for fun, like when they were kids in cheap hotels, shoving coins in the slot to make the Magic Fingers work.

"Sebastian," Viola had said, wide-eyed when he'd first brought her here, *"you don't need quarters for this one!"*

He crossed to her dresser. It was white and covered in stickers. Even the mirror was almost obscured by them. He pulled his gloves off and ran his fingers over the plastic veneer of the dresser. It was only cheap plywood underneath, but Vi had picked it out of a catalog as the one she wanted. It was covered in little trinket boxes. Henry opened one, and found hair bands with baubles inside. Strands of Vi's hair were tangled in the elastics.

He saw Viola's plastic ring, the gold paint flaking off it, and smiled. Smiled right through whatever seeing that did to his guts. He glanced in the mirror in time to see Sarah returning, another woman in tow. The second woman was about sixty—short with wide-set breasts that rested on a round stomach. Curly, woodchuck-brown hair set in tight curls. Fuchsia lipstick that bled slightly into the wrinkles around her lips. She wore a pink Winnie the Pooh sweatshirt over a red shirt. Her wrists were covered in bangles, and her earrings were two dangling miniature Pooh Bears with tiny honey pots.

All Henry could do was stare.

"Hell-o, Viola!" the woman trilled, violently cheerful. "You gave us all quite a scare." She turned to Sarah. "I'll take it from here."

Sarah left.

"Where did you go, young miss?" The woman shook her head, and her Pooh Bears wobbled.

Henry didn't answer. Viola sometimes had spells where she wouldn't talk to anyone. Henry thought staging one of those was his safest bet right now. The Technicolor nightmare leaned forward, her face inches from his. Her breath smelled like chili. Henry glanced at her name badge. *Dreama Carey Coleman. Volunteer Staff.*

"Now what are you grumpy for?" Dreama asked in that false-cheery voice. "If anyone should be grumpy, it's the people who didn't know where you'd gone. Who had to go looking for you. Wouldn't you agree, sweetie?"

Christ, if he'd had any idea Viola was in the clutches of this condescending maniac, he would have removed her from St. Albinus a long time ago. He stared at his hands.

"Well." Dreama straightened. "Dr. Carlisle will want to talk to you, but he's occupied now. And I'm a busy little bee as well. So how about this: you can take half an hour to shower and get changed and think about what we should tell Dr. Carlisle about our plan for keeping you out of trouble. You remember what we said last time? How you might need closer monitoring to cure those wanderin' blues?"

Henry's jaw tightened. Had they really threatened Vi with this Big Brother bullshit? He forced himself to nod.

"Half an hour," Dreama repeated. She pointed to the wall clock, which read quarter to twelve. "So when the big hand is on the three."

Henry really, really wanted to slap her. But he doubted that would help anything.

"You're a big girl, right? You can shower by yourself. You've been doing really well lately."

Of course Viola could fucking shower by herself. What the hell was this woman smoking? But he thought of times Vi forgot how to do things. How to make a sandwich, or how to button a shirt. She'd brush her front teeth, then stop without doing the back teeth. Most of the time she was fine. Just every now and then, she wasn't.

But that didn't give this Dreama lady the right to talk to Viola like a child. Henry balled his hands into fists and waited for her to leave. Then he glanced around the room. Half an hour. When the big hand hit the three. Showering was out of the question, not least of all because it would mess up his makeup. He waited three minutes, then opened the door. Peered out into the hall. Dreama was at the reception center in the front, talking to someone. He made one more check that the coast was clear, then hurried down the hall to the room where the name tag had been taken off. He opened the door and slipped inside.

The room was bare, the bed stripped of sheets. The dresser drawers were open and empty. Henry walked around. It was as if no one had ever been there. He wondered if he'd ever see Vi's room like that, stripped of anything that made it a home. He shivered.

In a small waste can by the bedside table, a green, turtle-shaped name tag was lying on a small pile of tissues and paper. Henry picked up the name tag and uncrinkled it. Bill Crowley.

On the table was a photo. Recent—February, according to the date stamp from the camera. Mr. Crowley, with his gray, wispy hair and hoard of wrinkles, standing by the Midwest Sports Complex with a younger man. The younger man was smiling, and Crowley almost was. The resemblance was clear—father and son. Had to be.

He left Crowley's room and headed down the hall. He'd have to cross the reception area to get to the offices, and the hub was bustling right now. Suddenly, a wail sounded from the room next to Crowley's. The name tag on the door was shaped like a dragon and read *Rodney Rhodes*. "They're coming!" a male voice yelled. "Chris! When I find Chris, I'll kill him. I'll kill him!"

Henry glanced around. If someone came to investigate the racket, they'd see him, so he hurried toward the reception area. In a moment of good fortune, a nurse spilled a tray she was carrying beside the front desk, and the other staff bent to help her clean up. He slipped across and into the opposite hall. There was a large copy room to his left, and then the hall turned to the right and became a corridor of offices.

These doors had official name plaques beside them, with braille lettering under the written names. He found Seth Carlisle's office, which had blinds partly covering the window. Henry stood to one side and peered in. Carlisle was at his computer. Henry flattened himself against the wall. Spied Mary Glanaham's office across the hall. Light on, door slightly open. No sign of anyone inside. He hurried in and went to the phone. All the speed dial numbers were labeled. He hit Carlisle, Number 2.

The man answered on the first ring. "Carlisle."

"Dr. Carlisle," Henry said. "This is Greg Frasier, the new volunteer?"

"What is it?" Carlisle snapped.

"Well, um, Rodney Rhodes in Room 102 seems to be having a—a hallucination. And he's getting kind of hysterical. I'm not really familiar with the procedure—"

"Get the on-duty nurse to give him a sedative."

"See, all the nurses are busy right now, and I was told it could be a while before anyone's available. And I'm *really* worried about Mr. Rhodes."

"Is he violent?"

"Um, no, but I think any minute now— Oh God, he's getting out of bed! Says he's going to find Chris and—"

"I'll be right there." Carlisle hung up.

Henry watched from Mary's office as Carlisle opened his door and stepped out, heading in the direction of the patient rooms. Then Henry darted inside Carlisle's office and pulled the door shut behind him, heading straight for the computer.

Carlisle's inbox was open. Henry scanned the subject lines and opened an email from the Berry, Kropf & Putzler law firm.

Dear Dr. Carlisle,

We are pleased to inform you that Bill Crowley's most recent will stands. The funds from Mr. Crowley's account will be transferred to St. Albinus next week. A discussion with Crowley Jr. this morning was productive, and I don't think he has any further plans to contest.

Best,

Tom Kropf
Berry, Kropf & Putzler
Attorneys at Law

Henry looked at the rest of the emails. Saw one from Dreama Carey Coleman two days ago, subject line: *Retirement*, and opened it.

It can be Rio or Ragsdale, as long as I'm with you.

-D

He scrolled down to the original email from Carlisle.

Where do you want to fly, angel?

A "most recent will" from Crowley? A transfer of Crowley's money to St. Albinus? Another Crowley contesting it? Crowley referring to Dreama as "angel"? Something was definitely afoot here.

He tensed as he heard the squeak of rubber-soled shoes in the hall. It was time to get the fuck out. He waited a moment, then opened the door and slipped into the hallway again. Turned left at the copy room and walked swiftly toward reception. He nearly bumped into a frazzled-looking staff member. "Sorry," he said in his normal voice, before remembering he was dressed as Vi. The guy didn't seem to notice.

Henry steeled himself to make the big cross. As he looked up to make sure the coast was clear, he stopped dead.

Standing at the front desk, talking to the receptionist, rubbing his bald head the way he did when he was agitated, was Special Agent Ryan McGuinness.

CHAPTER **FIVE**

"I'm here to see Viola Hanes." Mac hadn't been prepared for this at all. He'd triple-checked the address when he'd pulled up at the St. Albinus Care Center. Henry's sister was in a nuthouse?

Maybe he shouldn't have been so surprised.

"And what's your relation to Ms. Hanes, sir?" the receptionist asked.

"A friend of her brother's."

"All right, sir, if you'll just sign in . . ." The woman passed a clipboard to him. "She's in room 106."

In room 106. Not wandering the streets of Zionsville. So if Viola was back where she belonged, where was Henry?

Mac signed his name and headed down the hall to his right.

He knocked on the door to 106.

"Come in," said a soft voice.

When he entered room 106, Viola Hanes was lying with her back to him. She had on a large T-shirt and jeans with silver spangles on the back pockets. She was built just like Henry, that was for sure. Hair just a little lighter, and longer.

"Viola?"

"I was going to say sorry." Mac started at the voice, which was distinctly unfeminine—and incredibly familiar. "I was going to say I can explain everything." The figure on the bed rolled to face him. "But I think *you're* the one who needs to explain what the hell you're doing here."

"Henry." Because while the makeup was good, it was definitely Henry. Mac was too shocked to move, or to say anything else.

Henry sat up. "What are you doing here, Mac?"

He knew it was foolish, but he was a little disappointed Henry didn't seem glad to see him. In fact, Henry looked downright angry, which was ridiculous, because Henry was the one doing something stupid—not him.

He jarred his tongue loose. "Why are you in your sister's room at a mental hospital?"

"It's not a mental hospital!" Henry glared. "It's a care center. And I asked you first."

"I came to find out who Viola was."

Henry stood and approached him. Stood so close that the toes of his purple sneakers touched the tips of Mac's black loafers. And just like that, Mac was in love again. Lust. Whatever.

"Well, she's my twin sister, okay? And she's in a lot of fucking trouble, because this place is running some kind of scam, maybe even *killing* people. And I'm not leaving until I find out what's going on."

Mac sighed. He was an idiot. No amount of lust was worth the constant aggravation of dealing with Henry Page. Sebastian Hanes. Whoever. "Henry, if that's what you suspected—if you've got good *reason* to suspect it—then why the *fuck* wouldn't you tell the authorities?"

"Because Viola's scared!" Henry's voice was barely above a whisper, but it was fierce. "She left here because her friend in room 104 died suddenly. Under what I'm now convinced are fucking weird circumstances. I think the new director is extorting money from patients—one of the volunteers might be involved too. I wasn't going to bring Vi back here if it was dangerous."

"So where did you *put* her?"

Henry swallowed. His expression lost some of its ferocity. "With some friends."

"With some friends," Mac repeated, trying to keep his voice steady. "With your gang of criminals, you mean? A bit out of the frying pan and into the fire, isn't it? Especially when you have absolutely *no* proof that anyone here is—"

"Carlisle's emails," Henry interrupted.

"What?"

"Seth Carlisle. He's the new director. I went into his office—"

"Henry."

"Looked at his emails—"

"*Henry*."

"And found a message about Mr. Crowley—that's Vi's friend, well, *former* friend—having recently made a new will. A will leaving his money to St. Albinus. Somebody—I think his son—is contesting that. Or was, before someone shut him up. Why would Crowley leave his money to St. Albinus if he has a son?"

"Maybe they're estranged. Maybe—"

"There's a *recent* photo of them in Crowley's old room. They don't look estranged."

"How many rooms here have you been into?" he hissed.

"Just Carlisle's office and Crowley's room. Oh, and Mary Glanaham's office. Briefly. To use the phone."

He rolled his eyes. Heaven seriously fucking help him.

He was partly sympathetic. He'd had no idea Henry was dealing with a sister in long-term care, and he was impressed—*disguspressed*—by the lengths Henry was going in order to ensure she was safe.

But then a louder voice said, *No, this is just like Henry*. Claiming he had to go help someone in need, and now here he was in a wig and spangled jeans, lying, deceiving, breaking and entering, reading private emails...

"I should have figured," he said coldly. "I'd track you down, and what would you be doing but finding ways to make my life hell?"

"This has nothing to do with you. I didn't ask you to come here!"

"You're lucky I did come here before you got yourself in serious trouble!"

"Who do you think you are?" At some point Henry had gotten his face close enough to Mac's that he could feel little flecks of spit when Henry snarled at him. "Some kind of fucking overbearing mentor trying to get me to see the light? Fuck you! I'm not a good guy. This is what I do, and it's what I'm good at. And this is my sister we're talking about so *stay out of it*."

And then they were kissing, because fuck it.

Mac ran his fingers through Henry's wig. Pushed his hips against Henry's until Henry's knees buckled and he sighed into Mac's mouth. Henry squeezed Mac's shoulder and closed his eyes, his tongue sliding over Mac's.

They parted. "I hate you," Henry murmured.

"Sometimes I wish I hated you," Mac replied. Would have made things a lot easier.

"Yeah." Henry stroked his neck with his thumb. "That's it. I *wish* I hated you."

They kissed again, Mac sucking on Henry's tongue until Henry was rubbing against him. Henry gave short, staccato sighs, half-frustration and half-need, and he fidgeted more the longer Mac worked. Finally he laughed, pulling his tongue away.

"Okay." Henry stepped back. "I don't hate you. But Mac, some shit's not your business, all right?"

"And some shit's definitely not yours. Like Carlisle's emails."

Henry grinned. "But he's a shady old fuck. And I've got his number. You're kind of impressed, right? I mean, I've only been here half an hour."

Mac shook his head. "You're gonna need the good guys' help on this one."

"Do I have it?"

The door opened before he could answer. They took another step apart, and Mac tried to play it cool as a woman who looked like Cory's American Girl Samantha doll might at age sixty—curly brown hair, chipmunk cheeks, a tiny bow mouth, and dark, vacant eyes—entered. She wore a flat gold chain around her neck, and a Winnie the Pooh sweatshirt.

Mac hated Winnie the Pooh.

"Viola!" The woman's voice was cheery in a demented sort of way. "What's going on here? I thought you were going to shower by the time the big hand was on the three?"

"I have a visitor," Henry said in a high, soft voice.

"Oh!" the woman said, as though noticing Mac for the first time. "Hello. I'm Dreama. I'm a volunteer staff member. And you are?"

"Uh, Mac. I'm Viola's cousin." He immediately wanted to kick himself. Should have stuck with family friend. "Second cousin."

"Mm, oh!" Dreama nodded, her eyebrows raised. "How funny. Mr. Hanes never mentioned any living family."

"Well, there are a lot of things Mr. Hanes neglects to mention." He glanced at Henry.

"I haven't seen Cousin Mac in a long time," Henry said. And damn, he was good. His voice didn't sound like a falsetto imitation of a girl's at all. It sounded like the real thing.

"Well." Dreama smoothed the front of her sweatshirt. "Viola. I did want to let you know Dr. Carlisle may not be available to talk to you for another hour or so. Are you hungry now? When was the last time you ate, angel?"

"I'm not hungry." Henry had his hands folded strategically in front of his jeans. "I want to talk to Mac."

"Very well." Dreama cast a glance at both of them. "I'll be back later."

Dreama left the room. Mac walked to the door and closed it, then turned to Henry. "Who is *she*?"

"She's the one I think might be working with Carlisle."

"*Her*?"

"I know the Pooh is misleading..."

He grimaced. "I fuckin' hate Winnie the Pooh."

Henry started. "How do you hate Winnie the Pooh?"

"Are you serious?"

"Okay, the Disney-fied cartoon is awful, but the original books?"

"Hate him. And all his stupid friends. Especially Tigger."

"Aww, now Tigger. *Great* character."

"He..." Mac gestured to try to convey his disgust. "*Bounces*."

Henry slapped him on the shoulder and walked toward the bed. "Well, you know the wonderful thing about Tiggers is he's the only one."

"That's one too fucking many."

Henry sat on the bed. He looked . . . pretty. Beautiful. "Is it because they're talking animals and you only like realistic stuff?"

"It's because they're obnoxious."

"You like me. I'm obnoxious."

"The jury's still out on whether I like you."

"Aw, Mac." Henry leaned back on his hands. And spread his legs more than Mac thought was necessary. He looked—unless Mac was imagining it—a little hurt. "So, good guy. How are you gonna help me?"

"What do you need?" Mac couldn't believe he'd even asked, when the correct response was: *No, Henry. You're not a cop, this isn't an investigation, and I have real work I need to do.* Like a certain John Doe who'd been shot Rasnick style.

"I need all the info you can get on Seth Carlisle," Henry said. "And anything you can find on Dreama Carey Coleman. And I need stuff on the law firm of Berry, Kropf, and Putzler—anything regarding Bill Crowley's estate. I'll work on finding out if any other patients here have changed their wills recently."

"You're not going to stay here."

"I have to. They'll get suspicious if Viola goes missing again."

"They'll also get suspicious when they notice Viola's got an Adam's apple."

"You can barely see mine!" Henry put a hand to his throat.

"That doesn't mean you can keep this ruse up for long."

"I know." Henry extended his leg to nudge Mac's shin with his toe. "So you'd better hurry back with that information."

Mac didn't even bother to roll his eyes again. His exasperation only seemed to fuel Henry. "Henry?"

"Yeah?"

"Promise you won't do anything stupid."

"Anything you think is stupid, or anything I think is stupid?"

"Either. Both."

"It's a little late for that, Mac. Don't you think?"

Mac nodded and stared at the floor. "Yeah."

He would have liked another kiss before he went. But he settled for reaching out and ruffling Henry's . . . wig. "You get in trouble, call me."

He handed Henry a business card. And left.

Viola sat on the tweed couch in Stacy's house and watched Remy's card tricks.

She liked Remy. He was easy to talk to, and he didn't seem to think she was stupid. He smiled a lot, but there was something sad about him. Watching him was like watching a movie all lit in cool colors, with slow, quiet music, and you knew that even if the characters did some fun things together, it ultimately wouldn't be a movie that made you laugh.

Remy showed her how to sneak cards up her sleeve and then pull them out at the right moment without anyone noticing. Then he taught her to play poker, which made Viola go very still for a moment as a bitter, dark, lurching feeling snuffled around her mind. Because she *did* know how to play. She *had* known. And then that knowledge had fallen away.

There was a video game she and Sebastian used to play where you raced cars. One of the courses was a series of mountains, and huge chunks of rock fell from above and bounced on the track, and you had to weave around them or be crushed. That was how Viola imagined her brain—some big, crumbling thing that existed outside of her body. All she could do now was stare up at all she had once been, wondering if she was about to be crushed by all she was losing.

She could *feel* the moments she wasn't behaving right. Like demanding pink marshmallows in the café. That was little kid stuff. Or like telling Sebastian about the angel. Angels weren't supposed to be real. But this one was. Mr. Crowley had been afraid of it. He'd seen its shadow in his room. And now he was gone.

And Dreama said that angels were all around. That they watched you and then reported back to God if you were good or bad.

Viola wondered who reported back to God if the angels were bad.

She tried to pay attention to Remy and relearn poker. After a few hands, she started to get the hang of it.

"You've got a better poker face than Henry," Remy said. He was very thin and very pale. He was maybe even younger than Viola. His hair was black with red tips, and he had a metal ring in his lip and a bar in his eyebrow.

"Sebastian," she corrected.

Remy laughed. "Sebastian. Doesn't seem to fit a guy like that."

"It's from Shakespeare."

"Right. Sebastian and Viola. From the one with the storm. *The Tempest?*"

"No." Other people got things wrong, but no one thought they were stupid, or that they needed to be kept somewhere special, away from regular people. Sebastian said life wasn't fair. But that you had to learn to make the best of that unfairness. "*Twelfth Night.* There's a storm in that one too."

Remy grinned. "Shakespeare liked his storms."

"Sebby hates storms."

Remy's smile faded, and he shuffled the cards. "I know."

"I used to take care of him during storms, but I don't know who does now."

"I do, sometimes."

"Are you two in love?"

Remy paused for only a second before riffling the deck. He shook his head slowly.

"Why not?"

Remy glanced up. His eyes were greenish blue, like the plastic cup she'd used for brushing her teeth when she was little. Sebby'd had a blue one. Once he had accidentally used Viola's, and when she'd pointed that out to him, he'd said, *"They look basically the same."*

"But not exactly," she'd said.

"Well, you can't choose who you're in love with, right?" Remy shrugged. "Henry just doesn't feel it for me."

Which meant Remy felt it for Sebby. Viola stored that knowledge away, pleased and sad. Maybe she could tell Sebastian that Remy loved him. Sometimes it wasn't that you didn't love someone—it was that you were afraid they didn't love you back. And once you knew they did, it was easier to let yourself be in love with them. This thought came from somewhere distant—a horizon Viola was always trying to see past, where her adult self lived with a healthy brain and grown-up thoughts. Sebastian said sorry. He said it all the time, and sometimes Viola didn't know why, didn't know what he was sorry for. But every now and then, she thought maybe she did.

Stacy came in and looked for bread to make a sandwich. Viola studied her tattoos again. She had so many of them. Viola thought she might like to get a tattoo. The bread was moldy, but Viola told Stacy she could put peanut butter and jelly on crackers, and it would taste pretty good. Stacy went down the hall to see if Gerald had any crackers.

Remy was dealing another hand when Carson came out of the back lounge. That room had a TV like Viola's room at St. Albinus. And it smelled like smoke. There were couches and mattresses back there in case people needed to sleep over. Jo and Stacy were the only ones who had their own rooms. And Sebastian, though he let Remy sleep in his room when he was away. The only thing his friends weren't allowed to touch in his room was his locked drawer. Viola thought maybe that was where he kept the ring their mother had given him. She'd given Viola one too. A long time ago. They were cheap plastic; she'd gotten them out of a little dispenser outside a Chinese restaurant. She hadn't had enough quarters to get two, so she'd promised they'd come back. But Sebby had shown her how to trick the machine with a hairpin into giving them another ring. She'd warned him never to do that again, but she'd smiled, glad they could both have rings, just like Viola and Sebastian in *Twelfth Night*.

Viola still had hers in her box at St. Albinus. And Sebby's was probably in that drawer. She wished she could see. Maybe Remy knew Sebastian's hairpin trick and could get locked things open.

Carson grunted.

Viola didn't like Carson. He was old and had a mean face, and he stared too much. It wasn't polite to stare. He leaned against the living room doorway and watched them. Viola could see Remy's muscles tense, but he continued to deal. "All right, Vi," Remy said. "The wager."

"Remy." Carson's voice was quiet.

"'lo, Carson," Remy said, still not meeting his gaze. He looked at Viola instead and scooted some chips toward the center of the table. "Shall we play it dangerous?"

"Remy, you promised me something."

"I know, Carson. But I'm busy now."

"You want your cash or not?"

"Maybe later." Remy was trying to act like he didn't care what Carson was saying, but Viola could see how tense his shoulders were.

Carson shifted, his hands in his pockets. "I'll need more from you, for making me wait."

Remy finally looked up. "You know, I'm not actually that *hard up* right now." Anger made his voice rise. "So maybe you should forget it."

Stacy appeared in the hall behind Carson, a box of crackers in hand. "What's going on?" She pushed past Carson and into the kitchen area.

"Remy and I were just discussing his finances," Carson said. Viola hated his voice, low and clotted sounding. Hated his blank stare and the way he hefted his body around like every air molecule in the room belonged to him. And she hated how he grinned when he caught her watching him.

Stacy grabbed peanut butter from the cabinet. "Remy's doing some errands for me. I'll be paying him for it." She unscrewed the jar and jammed a knife in it, pulling out a massive glob of peanut butter. "So no need for you to lose any sleep over his finances." She was trying to sound casual, but Viola could tell she was angry too.

Carson remained in the doorway. "But you put limits on where he spends the money you give him, like he's a fucking child. You're not a child, are you, Rem?"

"Fuck off," Remy said, still studying his cards. "Both of you, fuck off. Viola and I are trying to play."

Stacy focused on her crackers. Carson said, "I'm going out."

"I don't need money from either of you," Remy said loudly. "I'll earn my own damn living and spend it however I want."

No one responded. After a moment, Carson crossed the living room. He squeezed Viola's shoulder as he passed. "Good luck, sweetheart. He plays dirty." He shut the door hard behind him, and Viola could hear his loud footsteps on the stairs. She twitched her shoulder, trying to shrug off where he'd touched her. Stacy went back to her room.

"I don't like him," Viola whispered.

"Nobody does." Remy leaned forward. "You know what, though? He thinks with his little head. And people like that are easy to control."

Viola laughed, though she wasn't sure what Remy meant. She waited for him to lay his cards down.

"Are you laughing at what I said, or is that the mirth of someone who knows she's won?" Remy asked.

"You'll just have to find out."

"You're a tough one to beat, Vi."

"I used to know how to play. Then I forgot after my accident. That was a long time ago." She suddenly couldn't stop talking, even though Sarah and Dreama at St. Albinus were always telling her not to say too much at once. "Sebby thinks he hurt me. But he didn't. The other man did. The man was hurting Sebby; just Sebby didn't want to say so. But

I can't talk to him about that. He feels bad even though I tell him it's okay. I know he didn't hurt me."

"Your brother," Remy said slowly, "has an odd tendency to believe he's hurt people when he hasn't. And to fail to notice when he actually has."

Viola set her cards down too. Sebastian must have hurt Remy a lot by not being in love with him. Once, in the hospital—not St. Albinus but a real hospital, a long time ago—Viola's roommate had been a boy who'd needed surgery to remove a tumor in his brain. Viola had liked him a lot. She'd made him a card. Later his friend had visited him, and Viola had heard them laughing about something, and then the boy said, *"The retarded girl gave it to me."*

Remy turned his cards over, and Viola did the same. She looked down and was embarrassed to realize the cards she'd played were completely random. They didn't mean anything when they were put together, and they certainly didn't beat Remy's flush. She pushed the chips at Remy.

"Did you play dirty?" she demanded.

"What?" He paused in gathering the chips.

"Did you play dirty, like he said?" Viola was suddenly very angry, but she wasn't sure why.

"No," Remy said softly, shaking his head.

"You played dirty." She said it loudly, meanly, and she said it even though she knew he hadn't played dirty—*she'd* played foolishly.

She got up and went to Sebastian's room, which was right beside Stacy's. She shut the door, and got down beside the dresser, rattling and pulling on Sebby's locked drawer until the knob broke off. Then she hurled the knob against the wall, flopped down on the bed, and stared at the ceiling.

CHAPTER SIX

St. Albinus. Mac couldn't stay away from the place. He was there the next morning, knocking on Henry's door. Ridiculous, because he had more to worry about than this little pantomime. There were OPR and John Doe, for starters. Hell, there were a hundred different things that should have been given higher priority than the Henry Page circus, but, somehow, here he was.

"Shit, Henry," he said in an undertone as Henry reappeared at last from Viola's small bathroom. "Seriously?"

Henry was wearing a summery dress that showed off his very shapely—and very shaved—legs.

"Viola," Henry reminded him in an undertone. "Have you called in Bosslady yet?"

"No." He tried to lift his gaze from the hemline that swung around Henry's knees. "For starters, you don't have a crime. And, if you did, it would be a matter for the local police, not the FBI."

"What do you mean I don't have a crime? The emails, hello?"

"That's a motive," Mac said. "And if we had an actual crime to go with it, it would be a damn good motive. But it's a big leap between Mr. Crowley leaving his money to this place, and Mr. Crowley getting murdered. You get that, right?"

"Shit, Mac, it's a classic! Call in the cops, throw in your patented glare, rough the bad guys up a bit, play the music, and let's get out of here!"

"What?" He rubbed his forehead. "What music?"

"You know. The music." Henry spread his fingers as though he was playing an imaginary piano. "The da-*dum*!"

"Are you doing the music from *Law & Order*?"

"Da-*dum*," Henry repeated. "Cue montage of crime scene photographs and newspaper headlines."

This was one of those moments—and there had been a lot—when Mac felt like he was watching two different Henrys. The manic, fun, reckless one who demanded attention with his outlandish behavior, and the other one. The one who tried to pass unnoticed in the background. The one who was afraid to get pinned down. The one who, when Mac looked at him too closely through all the smoke and mirrors, tried to hide. The real one?

"It's 'duhn-*duhn*,'" he said.

"It's 'da-dum,'" Henry insisted.

"'Da-dum' is like, Disney princesses doing chores with the help of woodland creatures. *Law & Order* is definitely 'duhn-duhn.'"

"Oh please." The light summer dress billowed as Henry twisted away. "God. Federal Bureau of Incompetence!"

"Henry," he said in a low voice, while Henry busied himself fixing his hair in the mirror. "Henry. *Sebastian*."

Henry's hand stilled, hovering over a glittery barrette. "Don't call me that."

"It's your name, isn't it?"

Henry fixed the barrette in place. "I suppose."

He didn't push it.

"I don't see how this doesn't concern the FBI," Henry said. "It's extortion."

"Where's the proof?"

"Who the hell leaves their money to the place where they spent twenty years of their life imprisoned and forced to eat weird pudding?"

"Weird pudding?"

"I had the pudding earlier, Mac. It was weird."

"Maybe Crowley liked it here."

"He hated it here." Henry smoothed his wig. "Though to be fair, he kind of hated everything. Especially the Japs."

Henry knocked over—Mac suspected on purpose—a package of stickers, and bent to pick them up.

Mac looked away. Looked back.

Henry was doing this on purpose. He wanted him to look. Or he wanted him to feel too uncomfortable to look. And Mac would be damned if he was going to give him that satisfaction.

He looked and kept looking. Henry was going to raise some suspicion with those legs. Yes, they were smooth—ungodly smooth—and yeah, they were slender, but they were muscled in a way he doubted the real Viola's were. He didn't know why Henry hadn't opted for jeans again. Except that Henry was stunning in that dress, and of course the dress provided easier access, which he should absolutely not be thinking about, because he wasn't here to grope Henry, and besides, those clothes belonged to Henry's sister, who was in long-term care. Should have been a boner killer.

Henry straightened and set the stickers back on the shelf.

"So what's . . ." He stopped. He'd almost asked, *What's wrong with Viola?* Probably not the best way to frame the question. "Has your sister been here a long time?"

Henry added a little more liner under his eyes. "Seven years."

"Has it helped?"

Henry met his gaze in the mirror. "She's not going to be cured, if that's what you're asking."

"I don't know what I'm asking. I don't know anything about her."

"That's probably for the best."

He picked at some lint on Viola's blanket. "So that's a 'shut up'?"

"Whatever the polite, fed-friendly version of 'shut up' is."

He nodded. "Little cool out for a sundress, isn't it?"

"I don't know. Pretty hot in here." Henry turned to face him. "I wasn't sure you'd come back."

"I said I'd get the information, didn't I?" Actually, he hadn't said that. But he'd gone and done Henry's bidding anyway. He wasn't sure he believed any of this stuff about Crowley and an extortion plot, but something was going on at St. Albinus that had Henry worried enough to place his sister in hiding. And Henry wasn't really the paranoid type. For all his seeming recklessness, Henry was careful about what he involved himself in.

"But you don't have any information. And you still came back to check on me."

"I do have information. I told you, I can't touch the law firm without sending up red flags. I'd need the Bureau's backing. And Carlisle's clean."

"One traffic ticket."

"Yep."

"And you're waiting on a callback from his previous employer?"

"Uh-huh."

"I don't think we have time to make polite inquiries, Mac."

"What sort of inquiries do you suggest we make? The kind where we tell Carlisle you looked at his emails, then slam his head into a table and ask if he stole Crowley's money?"

"Sounds good to me."

Henry's hands were on his hips. The shadows of his collarbone above the neckline of the dress made Mac swallow.

"Not a game, Henry," he warned.

Henry bent forward and placed his hands on his knees. Looked Mac in the eye. "I know that, Mac. My sister's involved. Don't you think I know that?"

"I think you want to do the right thing. And the right thing is stepping back and letting local authorities start an official investigation."

"The *right* thing is making sure this place is safe for Vi." Henry straightened. "We need to talk to Crowley's son."

"I told you, I couldn't find anything."

"They'll have his contact info in Crowley's file here. We just need to get ahold of that fi—" Henry fidgeted suddenly and put a hand up to his shoulder.

"Something wrong?"

"I think I broke a bra strap."

Mac watched Henry's fingers fiddle with the fabric of the dress. "Henry . . ."

Henry's eyes were large. For a moment, Mac didn't know if he was getting played or not; if that innocent-but-needy look was intentional, or if Henry was showing his real face for once.

He cleared his throat. "I talked to a contact in the Zionsville PD."

"You did?"

"There was no autopsy on Mr. Crowley," he said.

"That's suspicious, right?"

"Not necessarily. He was old, and he wasn't in great health, and the family didn't ask for one. His regular doctor signed off on it. Do you know what renal failure is?"

"When the renal doesn't work anymore?"

Mac snorted. "Anyway, Mr. Crowley was sick and old, and he died."

"What?" Henry flicked a length of hair over his shoulder, and dug his fingers into the neckline of his dress. "So you came all this way to tell me that you're not going to help me?"

"I *did* help you," he said firmly. "That thing where I called people and asked questions? That was helping you. But there's not a crime here. Look, if you need to do this to prove to yourself that this place is still right for your sister, then I think you're crazy, but I *get* it. And maybe the pudding tastes weird and maybe you don't like the lady in the Winnie the Pooh sweatshirt, and maybe it just plain sucks that Viola has to stay in a place like this, but that doesn't make it a crime scene, okay?"

He half expected Henry to say something crazy. Instead, Henry dropped his gaze, and Mac felt a strange surge of guilt for ripping the wind out of his sails like that.

"Why'd you come back then?"

Mac wasn't entirely certain himself. "To make sure you were still here. To make sure you're not going to vanish instead of testifying. And to bring you back your stuff."

He gestured to the plastic bag he'd left lying on the floor. Henry's belongings from the hotel in Indianapolis. A few items of clothing and his book of Shakespeare.

"Thanks," Henry said, still not looking at him. He picked up a plastic ring from Viola's dresser and turned it over in his palm. When he spoke again, his voice was soft, but close to breaking. "She looked after me, Mac. I gotta do the same for her."

"Come here," Mac said, and didn't wait for him to respond. He took a step to close the distance between them, and wrapped his arms around Henry. Whatever had happened in his past, with his juvie record, with Viola, however it had shaped him, none of it mattered now. Henry needed someone, and Mac was here. It was allowed to be that simple, wasn't it? He rubbed Henry's back gently. "So who looks after you now?"

Henry breathed against his neck. Mumbled something dissenting, but didn't pull away.

He even smelled like a girl. Mac couldn't help inhaling deeply to catch more of the scent: a citrusy summery fragrance. And Henry just stood there, unresisting, leaning into his embrace as though he really did need it. A dangerous fantasy, for both of them.

Mac slid his hands lower, rubbing the fabric of the dress over the knots in Henry's spine. Cupping one hand around Henry's ass, and pulling him closer. Heat pooled in his groin as he felt Henry's erection pressing against him. That was one thing the thin dress couldn't hide.

He widened his stance, and Henry shifted so that he was half-straddling Mac's thigh. He tilted his head and licked a line up Mac's throat, before sighing against his ear. "Pretty sure I won't be able to explain a mess like that in my laundry, Mac."

"I'll take your laundry with me when I go."

Henry rocked against him. "I'm trying real hard not to think about the fact that I'm wearing Viola's underwear."

Mac snorted and made a face.

"Sorry." Henry leaned back, putting his arms around Mac's neck. "Mood killer, right?"

He pretended to consider that for a moment. "Well, I don't know Viola. So I might be okay with it."

Henry's smile was hesitant. "Yeah, sorry, it's a bit too weird."

"Weirder than the pudding?"

"It said it was banana, Mac. But it didn't taste anything like banana."

Mac shook his head. "You're something else, Henry Page."

Sebastian Hanes.

He wondered if there would ever be a time when Henry would let him call him by his real name. Wondered why Henry hated to hear it so much.

Henry let him go and stepped back. He adjusted his dress, sighing at the way his erection tented the fabric. "I think I'm gonna need a long shower tonight, Mac."

"Need anyone to wash your back?"

Henry's eyes darkened. "When I leave here, when Viola's safe, I'll take you up on that. You can wash my back, and then I'll suck you so hard you won't be able to walk straight."

"Henry," he said. "Don't make me walk past the nurses' station with a hard-on, please."

"Turnabout's fair play." Henry adjusted his dress again. "And then, when you've recovered the power of speech, we'll talk about who's topping and who's bottoming."

Mac raised his eyebrows.

"What?" Henry twirled, the dress floating out. "You think just because I'm dressed like a girl that I'm automatically the bottom?"

"Not at all," Mac said. "I was just wondering why we needed to discuss it when we could just toss a coin to see who goes first."

"I like it when you surprise me, Mac. Not very many people surprise me." Henry grinned and turned around. "Now, help me with my bra?"

He slipped his hand down the back of Henry's dress. "It's not snapped. It's come off its little hook thingy. Why is there a little hook thingy?"

"It's a convertible bra," Henry said, sweeping his hair off his neck. "You can take the straps off it and wear it with a strapless dress, or do a crossover thingy for dresses with shapes cut in the back."

"Why are you wearing such a complicated bra?"

"I borrowed it off a friend. It was the only one she had spare."

Mac tried to catch the plastic loop on the hook, and missed. "This is ridiculous."

Henry reached up to cup his hands over his fake breasts, which were being jerked from side to side as Mac struggled with the strap.

"Those," he said, "are very convincing, by the way."

"I think they're silicone," Henry said. "They feel weird. Wanna poke them?"

"No thanks."

Henry jabbed a finger into one. "If I was a girl, I'd probably poke my boobs all the time."

Mac rolled his eyes. "I bet you wouldn't."

"No." Henry pressed back against Mac, his ass rubbing against his crotch. "I'd find some nice, big FBI guy to poke them for me."

"Well, you're barking up the wrong tree here, young lady," Mac said, trying for a severe tone and completely fucking it up.

"Oh, am I, Officer?" Henry sighed theatrically. "It's not my boobs you want to poke, is it? But I'll have to warn you, if you try and take my underwear off, you're in for a big surprise."

Mac dipped his head forward and nipped Henry's throat. "Stop. Teasing. Me."

"Or what?" Henry asked, his eyes half-closed and his voice low.

"Or I'll throw you down on that bed and show you exactly how much I don't care for these." He slid a hand down the front of Henry's dress and squeezed a fake breast through the fabric of the bra. "And I'd make you come so hard that you actually shut your mouth for five minutes."

"Mmm." Henry wiggled. "Sounds like fun, Agent McGuinness. But first let's get my boobs sorted out."

Mac withdrew his hand, just as Henry's door swung open.

The lady in the Winnie the Pooh sweatshirt gawped at them.

Which was when Mac realized he was pressed up flush against the backside of a mentally disabled woman, one hand on her waist and the other on her shoulder, and her bra strap was hanging out of her rumpled dress.

Whoops.

"Viola!" Dreama exclaimed. "What on earth is going on here?"

Henry straightened up. "What?"

Dreama squared her shoulders. Her sweatshirt stretched across her ample bosom, giving Pooh a disturbing leer, which effectively killed Henry's hard-on. "Viola, go to the common room and wait for me there. I need to speak to your cousin in private."

"Second cousin," Mac said.

"Bye, Mac." Henry didn't dare meet his gaze in case he burst out laughing. He trailed out the door, and then leaned against the hallway wall to listen.

"Now, I don't know exactly what was going on here," Dreama said in a voice that belied that. "But your behavior was highly inappropriate! Viola is a very special young lady, and she might have the same needs and urges as any other young woman, but I won't allow her to be taken advantage of, do you understand?"

"Yes."

Henry wrinkled his nose. He didn't really want to hear Dreama talk about his sister's needs and urges. He knew all about them. Years ago, when he'd tried to look after her himself, he'd caught her inviting a man back to their apartment. Some slimy neighbor whose idea of talking dirty was to tell her exactly how hard he'd pound her and pull her hair. And Viola had smiled and nodded as though he was offering her a day at the park instead of rough sex.

"Why can't I, Sebby?" she'd screamed at Henry after he threw the guy out. *"Why can't I?"*

Because your brain hasn't caught up with your biology, Vi. Because it never will.

"Viola can't make an informed decision in regards to... to matters of the heart," Dreama said now.

Henry hated the euphemism almost as much as he hated the alternative.

"Her hair was caught in her bra strap," Mac lied, his voice even. "That's all that happened. She's my *cousin*."

Second cousin, Henry thought with a slight smile. And Mac really was gay if he'd never had enough experience with bras to know that getting your hair caught in them was a near impossibility. He'd also obviously never hung around many girl friends or drag queens either. Still, Henry admired the way he delivered the lie.

"I'll speak to Dr. Carlisle about this." Dreama gave a little huff. "You'll need to talk to him before you come and visit again, young man. I wasn't born yesterday, you know."

No. Henry was pretty sure she was born when dinosaurs ruled the planet.

"That's fine," Mac said. "And I will be back to visit Viola. Tomorrow. So Dr. Carlisle had better make the time to see me."

He stormed out of Viola's room, almost colliding with Henry.

"My hero," Henry whispered, blowing him a kiss and hurrying down the hall toward the common room before Dreama saw him.

Mac was coming back tomorrow.

Mac might not believe him, but he was coming back tomorrow.

And if that didn't earn him the gift of the macaroni necklace Henry was making in craft class, he didn't know what did.

"McGuinness," Mac said into his phone as he drove back to the city. He was still smarting over being treated like a pervert by a woman in a Pooh sweatshirt.

"Mac, it's Penny."

"What's up?" Mac overtook a minivan that was going two miles under the speed limit. Why was the world full of irritating assholes today? And why was Henry Page their king?

"Val wants to know where you are."

"Did you tell her I'm on lunch?"

"Yes. She wants to know why you've been on lunch for almost two hours when you're supposed to be on sick leave."

"You phoned to tell me that?" Val knew the score. He was on sick leave because he wanted to get all his ducks in a row before he dealt with OPR. It certainly didn't mean he was going to stay home, lie on his couch, and watch daytime TV. Not when there was work to be done.

"No, I phoned to tell you that we've got an ID on John Doe," Penny said.

Mac felt a buzz of anticipation. He gripped his phone tighter. "Who is he?"

"Lonny Harris."

Mac gave it a moment, but no. Nothing. "I have no idea who that is."

"No," Penny agreed. "Me neither."

CHAPTER SEVEN

Barbara Eiling, the previous administrator for St. Albinus, now managed an assisted-living facility in Topeka. Mac called her and asked flat-out why she'd left St. Albinus.

"Well, the church sold it," she told him. "They've kept the name, but it's now owned by one of those corporations that puts profits before people."

"Is that why you left?" He checked his watch. He had about twenty minutes before he was due to meet Penny in the parking lot so they could go and check out where Lonny Harris's body had been found. Penny was currently getting information sent over from the police, and Mac couldn't help but think that would have been a better use of his time than this. But he'd promised Henry he would make some calls.

"I had . . ." Barbara paused while she searched for the right word. "I had *issues* with some of the new board's policies. They started by dropping the wages of the staff, and then told us to save money by reusing paper cups."

"Paper cups?" Mac was confused.

"It's the principle of the thing," she told him. "Once they start citing paper cups as a way to cut the budget, you know it's going to get a hell of a lot worse. And sooner or later, usually sooner, there is a decline in patient care. I've been there before, and I didn't want to watch it happen again. To be perfectly honest, I jumped before I was pushed. I refused to take a pay cut as well."

Mac brought up the St. Albinus website on his computer. It looked so pretty in the pictures. Residents walked in the gardens, and smiled for the cameras . . . Meanwhile someone was counting up how many paper cups they used.

"But I don't think you called me to talk about paper cups."

"I'm actually looking into the recent death of one of the patients," he said. "It's just routine."

"Oh, which one?"

"Mr. Crowley."

She surprised him with a laugh. "Oh God, I'm sorry. It's just I figured he'd live forever. He was a real curmudgeon. I thought he'd be around to torment his caretakers for years yet."

"He died of renal failure,"

"He had chronic kidney disease," Barbara said. "Still, he was only in stage one when I left a few months ago. It must have progressed very quickly."

Mac was silent for a moment. Maybe Henry's ideas weren't all crazy. Apart from the one about dressing as his twin sister, of course. That was soap opera shit. Pretty soon the villain everyone thought was dead would reappear in a dramatic thunderstorm.

He shook his head and refused to think of Jimmy Rasnick rising from the grave.

"Oh." Barbara breathed out slowly. "Routine? No, you think this is an Angel of Death situation."

"It's just routine. I really can't tell you any more than that. I also wanted to ask about another of your former patients, Viola Hanes."

"Viola? Is she okay?"

"She's fine," Mac said. "She was close with Mr. Crowley?"

"They were like two peas in a pod. It was crazy, really. This terrible, cranky old man, and this girl with the mental age of an eight-year-old. And both of them could throw tantrums like you wouldn't believe, but they got on so well together."

"Who pays for Viola's care?"

"Her brother," Barbara said. "Sebastian."

"And what does he do for a living?" Mac was curious as to what Henry had told them.

"I . . . I never actually asked."

Mac smiled at her hesitation. She might not have asked, but she suspected something was wrong.

"Look," Barbara said, "Vi didn't have insurance. She didn't have some big compensation payout for her injury either. But the money was there, every month."

"And how much money was it?"

"Five thousand three hundred per month."

"Shit. Pretty sure she could rent an apartment in New York for that amount."

"No. Not Viola. She needs around-the-clock care. She has both medical and behavioral issues. She's a sweet girl, but she can't be on her own. I know her brother tried to look after her at first, but he couldn't. I don't know which one of them was more heartbroken when she was admitted with us."

"Is that why you didn't ask where the money came from?"

"She needed us." Barbara's voice was soft. "And so did he."

"How long has she been there?"

"Seven years."

He tried to imagine that. Tried to imagine Henry—Sebastian—at eighteen. Tried to imagine a kid of that age struggling to look after his sister on his own. And tried to imagine exactly how far he'd go to earn over five grand a month.

Except he didn't need to imagine, did he? He knew what Henry was. A criminal.

A criminal who carried all his earthly possessions in a plastic bag because every cent he made went to Viola.

"Thanks for your help," he told Barbara, and ended the call.

He glanced at his watch again. Shit, he didn't have time to look into Dr. Seth Carlisle and the new management of St. Albinus right now. But he could absolutely delegate it.

Mac headed outside to look for Dennis.

And ran into Janice Bixler.

"Hello, Viola," Dr. Seth Carlisle said with a smile. He peered at Henry over his glasses. "Now, you and I need to have a little chat. Is that okay?"

Patronizing fuck.

Henry sat down and stared at his lap. Let his hair fall in front of his face as he twirled the beaded bracelet on his wrist. "Okay."

"Now, we all got very worried when you ran off the other day. You know that you're not allowed to leave the grounds, don't you?"

"Yes."

"Is it because you're upset about Mr. Crowley?"

He shrugged.

"Okay. Well, it's perfectly normal to be upset when a friend goes away. I'm sure that Mr. Crowley would have wanted to say good-bye, but he was just very, very sick."

Was this the sort of shit they fed the patients here? Viola wasn't a child. She knew what death was. They didn't have to sugarcoat it for her.

"Now, Dreama tells me that you've had a visitor as well." Dr. Carlisle looked at his notes. "Your cousin Mac?"

"Second cousin," Henry said.

"You're not supposed to have visitors that aren't on the list." Dr. Carlisle set the notes aside. "Even family. Next time Mac comes, we'll have to tell him that he can't see you unless Sebastian puts his name on the list."

He tilted his head. "Okay."

Five minutes alone with a fax machine should sort that little problem out. He'd fax a letter of authority to Mac, have him chop the St. Albinus header off, and resend it. Hopefully not from the Indianapolis FBI field office. Because, awkward.

Or he could go and write a letter now, and slip it to Mac when he arrived. Because who was to say that Sebastian and cousin Mac hadn't met up for coffee that very morning? He wondered if Viola had any paper in her room that wasn't covered in ponies or rainbows. She liked pretty things.

He felt the familiar twist in his guts. The guilt. The self-disgust. He'd only done it for the money, he'd told himself a thousand times, but it wasn't true. He'd done it because he was too scared to refuse. Because he didn't want his mother to find out what her boyfriend was doing. It was sick, and dirty, and he was just a fucking weak crybaby like J.J. said, but the money made it feel . . . not better, but it made him feel as though he was stronger somehow, that he was colder. That it was a transaction, not an assault. The money made him feel that he was an accomplice, not a victim. And he might have kept on believing it, if only Viola hadn't heard one night and come crashing in to save him.

"Are you even listening to me, Viola?"

He glanced up at Dr. Carlisle's craggy face, and seethed with anger. Even if Carlisle hadn't done anything to Mr. Crowley, he was a bastard. Talking down to him as if he were a kid. Did he treat all his patients like this, or just Viola? "Sorry," he said softly. "I won't run away again."

"See that you don't." Dr. Carlisle drummed his fingers on his desk. "It's a privilege for you to stay here, Viola. Your brother pays good money to let us care for you. You don't want to disappoint him, do you?"

"No," Henry murmured, hating the man more every second. "I don't want that."

"Good." Dr. Carlisle's thin mouth turned up in a smile. "That's a good girl."

Patronizing fuck.

"Agent McGuinness." Janice Bixler was coolly polite. "I was told you were on leave." She glanced at the place where Mac had been shot. Even though the wound was covered, she seemed to know exactly where it was.

"But you thought you'd check my office, just in case?" He knew it was playing with fire to cop an attitude with OPR, but he couldn't help himself.

"Are you on leave, or aren't you?"

"I am. But I stopped by the office to check the progress on a couple of cases."

"Then you won't mind if I ask you a few questions?"

Yes, I fucking mind. He checked his watch. Fifteen minutes until he was supposed to meet Penny.

"Somewhere to be?" she asked.

Mac stepped back and gestured to his office. "Not at all."

"It's about Lonny Harris." Bixler stepped past him, into the office.

He closed the door behind them, with the distinct feeling he'd just sprung a trap shut on himself. "Lonny Harris?"

Bixler turned. "That name mean anything to you?"

It hadn't an hour ago. He hesitated probably a half a second—which was still too long. "I don't know who that is."

No way was he showing his hand before Bixler showed hers. Not that he had much of a hand, but every instinct told him to trust Bixler only as far as he could throw her. She was here to crucify someone, and Mac had a feeling he was at the top of her list.

"Interesting." Bixler took a seat in front of his desk and crossed her legs. "I was given to understand you were very much aware of Lonny Harris."

Now what the hell did that mean? He rubbed his aching chest.

"Valerie Kimura tells me that you were appraised of the file on the John Doe that was found shot in the head and the chest."

Thanks for the heads-up, Val.

"Are you telling me that my John Doe is called Lonny Harris?" Shit, he really hoped Bixler hadn't talked to Penny. "If that's the case, I still don't recognize the name."

"Lonny Harris was a piece of shit," Bixler snapped, leaning forward. "A thief, an addict, and an all-around waste of oxygen." She settled back. Took a breath. "He was also an informant."

"Whose?"

"Mine," Bixler said pleasantly. "And, because of course you've never heard of him, you didn't know that, right?"

"Right." Mac clenched his jaw.

"Lonny Harris dealt coke."

"And?" Mac was at a loss to understand where this was going.

"He claimed you were a pretty regular customer."

Mac might not have known what to expect, but it sure as fuck wasn't this. "That's *ridiculous*!"

Bixler stared at him. "Calm down, Agent."

"I never—"

"He said you got rough with him one night when you thought he'd screwed you over."

"For fuck's sake!" Mac couldn't get his voice down, though he knew yelling wasn't doing him any favors. "You're gonna believe the word of some fucking scumbag—"

"*Agent McGuinness*," Bixler said, "we are taking this very seriously, given your penchant for—shall we say excessive force?"

"*Shall we say . . .?*" Mac mocked. "No we shall not say. I want to know where on my record it says—"

"Louie Gallo," Bixler said. "No formal disciplinary action, but there was a hearing—"

"Gallo fought like an animal. An *animal*. It was me or him. Anyone'll tell you that. Val will tell you that."

"Jimmy Rasnick," Bixler continued. "His wife said you brutalized him during his arrest."

Mac heard again the sound of Rasnick's head hitting the wall. "I did what was necessary to get my perp under control. If the Bureau had a problem with it, they would have investigated."

"Well, Agent McGuinness, I'm investigating now." Bixler crossed her legs. "You and your partner, Agent Kimura, were both candidates for a promotion after that bust. She got it. Even though *you* made the arrest."

"She deserved it. She was the one who got Rasnick where we needed him."

"Are you sure that's why she got it?"

"What other reason would there be?" Mac asked, voice cold.

"I've spoken to former AD Sullivan. Who said the Bureau had to discipline you somehow. So it was good-bye to any hope of Special Agent in Charge McGuinness."

She was lying. Val would have gotten the promotion no matter what.

Somewhere, a jealousy Mac had always tried to pretend didn't exist showed its head. He *had* wanted the promotion. He'd been a fucking *hero* in the Rasnick bust. Not some fucking local pig who played dumb on the difference between subduing a perp and beating the shit out of him.

"So, Agent," Bixler went on. "You can see why we want to look into Harris's claims."

"I have *never* heard of anyone named Lonny Harris. And you really think I'm—what, a coke addict?" Mac laughed. "All of my drug tests are clean, my record is clean . . ."

"I don't know that I'd call it clean, Agent McGuinness. Louie Gallo. Jimmy Rasnick. The cabin in Altona. And given the recent reports of your erratic behavior—"

"What reports?"

"Your coworkers have mentioned mood swings. Temper tantrums."

His diet. His fucking doctor-recommended, no-sugar, no-carbs, no-coffee, no-alcohol, no-joy diet. Yeah, he'd been a bastard over the last few weeks. But what sane person would jump to the conclusion he was using drugs?

Bixler wasn't sane, though. She and Dreama Carey Coleman could have started a fucking coven of crazy together.

"I was giving up coffee," he told Bixler, aware he sounded defensive. "You ever given up caffeine before?"

"I don't drink coffee." Bixler glanced at her watch. "Careless mistakes—you let your witness walk away from a crime scene. Then you lost him a second time. Let him walk out of this office."

"That witness—" Mac began, but stopped. *I'd like to see you hold on to him for more than five minutes.*

Bixler tilted her head. "Where is that witness, Agent?"

"I'm not his jailer. He's free to move about town."

"You seem so . . . *close* to Henry Page. Yet you have no way of contacting him?" Her voice was low. And the way she said the word "close" made Mac queasy.

"None right now," Mac said, making sure there was an edge to his tone. "And I'm not going to say another word to you without a lawyer present."

"All right then." Bixler rose. She seemed oddly satisfied. "That's a good idea. And I hope you'll be able to produce that elusive witness of yours. Since you're so sure he can corroborate your version of what happened in Altona."

"I can't believe you're wasting my time with this crap."

"Lonny Harris was killed just before he prepared to lodge an official complaint against you. That's very convenient." She straightened her jacket. "I don't think it's nonsense."

"Anyone here would speak up for me." Mac hoped that was true. So far all they'd apparently spoken up about were his caffeine-withdrawal symptoms. Fuckers.

Maybe this was why Henry had suggested he make friends with his coworkers. So that when the opportunity arose to throw him under a bus, they didn't line up, jostling to be first.

"The best thing you can do right now is cooperate fully. Find that witness." She smiled tightly. "Have a good day, Agent McGuinness."

She was out the door before Mac could figure out how to move again.

Fuck her and the phony color-of-law complaint she'd ridden in on.

Mac really didn't have time for this. He texted Penny, took two Tylenol, grabbed his jacket, and headed out.

Lonny Harris's body had been found behind an abandoned building just off Capitol Avenue. Mac's shoes crunched over broken glass as he inspected the small yard.

Paper fluttered in the breeze as Penny opened the report.

"Okay," she said, squinting into the sun. "Going by the photos, the body was found over there, against that wall."

They headed over.

It was strange. Mac knew there wasn't anything to find; the local police had already been over the crime scene. But visiting the location was important for more than collecting physical evidence. It gave Mac a feel for the dimensions of the place. It gave him better perspective.

Not that he could concentrate on anything but what Agent Bixler had told him.

It's bullshit. I didn't know Lonny Harris; he didn't know me.

He and Penny walked around for a while.

Penny was doing her best not to bounce, but there was a spring in her step she couldn't hide. She was recovering from shoulder surgery, and had been deskbound for a lot longer than Mac. She was stir-crazy, and being outside at an actual crime scene was obviously like Christmas. She couldn't stop smiling. Mac almost expected her to burst into song.

It was worth the risk of getting busted by Val.

And the risk of getting caught sniffing around the murder of someone who'd apparently had it in for Mac.

He'd made absolutely sure he hadn't been followed here. Might have looked kind of funny, him going straight from an interview where he'd all but had Harris's death pinned on him to the scene of Harris's murder. The last thing he needed was to give Janice Bixler any more ammunition.

But part of him was glad he was doing this. It wasn't illegal, and fuck Bixler and her bullshit. It was more important than ever to find out why Lonny Harris had been killed. And by whom.

"One exit," Penny said, pointing toward the busted gate that led into the alley. "But nothing to suggest he was chased in here. He was probably meeting someone."

Mac looked up at the back wall of the abandoned building. The windows were broken, and plastic had been taped over them. Squares of it had torn partially free on several of the windows, and snapped like sails in a high wind. Walls rose on the other two sides of the yard.

"Who owns the building?"

"A Chinese company," Penny said. "They're buying up everything in the block to knock down and build a mall. No link to Rasnick or any of his known associates that I could find."

He was impressed that she'd already checked it out. He hadn't worked with Penny much in the past, but she had a reputation for efficiency. He supposed she needed it, being blonde and pretty. There were probably a lot of assholes who looked her up and down and assumed they knew why she got the job. He'd seen some of the same prejudices at play when he'd been partnered with Val.

Val, who had been promoted above him and currently thought Penny and Mac were out picking up lunch, and definitely *not* checking out a crime scene on their own.

"The report puts time of death at around four in the morning," Penny said. "The body was discovered at 9 a.m. by some kids playing hooky, and it had rained. Heavily. Washed away most of the physical evidence."

"So what have we got?" Mac studied the ground, as though it might somehow tell him. "Lonny Harris, last known address in

Greenwood. So who the hell was he meeting here at 4 a.m.? And how is he connected to Jimmy Rasnick?"

And how the fuck is he connected to me*?*

Harris was hardly a criminal heavyweight. He had a few previous arrests for selling stolen property, some drug offenses, and he'd done a couple of months in prison. There was nothing in his history that leaped out and screamed an association with Jimmy Rasnick.

If Lonny's death was a message, it was an obscure one.

"I'm getting his phone records sent over from Homicide. Maybe they missed something." Penny squatted down. "Hey, I found a quarter."

"Must be your lucky day."

Penny looked at him curiously, almost as though she was searching for sarcasm.

Shit. Was he really that unlikable? He'd always thought of himself as professional, until Henry had kindly pointed out that in his case, professional meant the same as friendless. So what if he didn't know every little detail about his colleagues' partners or kids or softball tournaments or favorite colors or horoscopes or brands of toothpaste? How was any of that *necessary*? He worked with these people, he wasn't trying to get into a green card marriage with them.

Penny smiled at last. "I guess it is." She slipped the quarter into her jacket pocket and wiped her hands on her pants.

Mac looked around the yard again. "When we get back, I need you to go through all Harris's phone contacts. Run their names and see if anyone stands out. And keep it under your hat, okay?"

Penny nodded, her expression suddenly wary.

Mac didn't dare spell it out for her. She either had his back or she didn't.

He checked his watch. "Shit. I'm supposed to be somewhere."

He was supposed to be in Zionsville, reminding Henry not to do anything stupid. Zionsville, where there was still no evidence of a crime at all, unless Henry's instincts had been right. The whole thing was starting to appear more and more suspicious and, after talking with Barbara Eiling, Mac knew Henry was right about one thing: Viola would be better off living somewhere else.

"Um..." Penny frowned.

"What?"

She drew a deep breath. "You're supposed to be at a doctor's appointment, right? Because that's what I'm going to tell the boss when she asks where you are and reminds us to play by the book now that OPR is sniffing around."

"Right." Mac was relieved. She had his back. "A doctor's appointment."

Penny flashed him a smile. "Yeah, that's what I thought."

They headed to the car.

"I'm sorry," the cheery woman in the frighteningly vivid sweatshirt told Mac. "You're not authorized to see Viola, and Dr. Carlisle is much too busy to see you."

Stymied by Dreama Carey Coleman.

He wondered if he should just flash his badge, but if Henry was right about this place, that would be a mistake.

"Ten minutes?"

"I'm sorry," Dreama trilled smugly.

Mac glowered. "Fine." He glanced down the corridor, and saw a figure flitting along. A figure in a floral baby-doll dress. *Shit*. How wrong was it that Henry looked so fucking good like that? Drag had never done anything for him, and neither had girls. So what the hell was it with Henry in a dress that made Mac want to bend him over the nearest flat surface and pound him into next week?

Henry tapped his wrist, then splayed his fingers and pointed at the front door. Five minutes?

Mac pulled his gaze back to Dreama before she noticed the pantomime playing out over her fuzzy shoulder. "Fine. I'll come back later."

"Visiting hours are between ten and twelve, and then two and six."

"For a place so concerned with security, you don't do a great job keeping tabs on your residents."

Dreama pursed her lips. "If you want to speak with someone from security, I can call them now." She fiddled with a plastic tag around her neck. A panic button.

Making veiled threats like that, she could have had a great career interrogating suspects.

"Fine," he said again. He turned and left the reception area, scowling at a startled orderly on his way out.

Outside in the parking lot, he checked his watch. And Henry, true to form, appeared around the side of the building exactly four and a half minutes later. He gestured wildly to Mac, and Mac crossed the parking lot.

"Had to crawl out the kitchen window," Henry said. He shoved a folded piece of paper into Mac's hands, beaming.

"What's this?"

"It's my letter of authority to let second cousin Mac visit Viola." Henry looked as if he was about to burst with pride, like some little kid with a gold star and an elephant stamp on his book report.

Mac slid it into his pocket.

"What? Aren't you going to use it?"

Mac snorted. "You're kidding, right? What, I've had this all along, and it just slipped my mind five minutes ago?"

Henry rolled his eyes. "Confidence, Mac. It's all about *confidence*."

"As in, con man?"

Henry's smile faltered for a second, but then blazed brighter than before. "Absolutely. There's a park across the street. Let's talk."

Mac walked with him, casting furtive glances back at St. Albinus. Now that he'd been painted as the potentially depraved and definitely gropey second cousin, he didn't want anyone to see him walking away with Viola. Because getting taken down by security, or worse, the cops, would make for a fun conversation. Particularly the part where he explained he was totally innocent because Henry was a guy masquerading as his own twin sister, and yes, Mac had knowingly let him do it. And even lied to keep Henry's cover intact. OPR would love that, wouldn't they? Helping a known con man set up in a facility full of vulnerable people? That would not look good. Not from any perspective.

"Henry," he said as they entered the park, "it's gotta stop."

Henry turned to face him, his dress floating out and showing off his thighs. "What does?"

Mac gestured at him. "*This*. All of this. Look, we could both get in a lot of shit for your little unauthorized investigation. What you're doing here is *illegal*."

And I'm in enough trouble already.

Henry's brow creased. "And so is what they're doing. It's illegal too, but it's much worse than me wearing a dress."

"Leave," he said. "Find somewhere else to put your sister, and then make a real complaint to the police and let them investigate it."

"There's nowhere else," Henry said. "Do you know what waiting lists are like, Mac? I can't move her, not anywhere permanent, so I have to make sure it's safe here, okay?"

"Even if it's not—"

"If it's not," Henry said, his voice hardening, "then I'll make sure it fucking is!"

"If you're right about this place, then what you're doing is worse than illegal, it's *dangerous*." Mac sighed. "You can't just . . . you can't just *do* this. There are rules. There are processes. You can't just do whatever the hell you want."

Henry stared at him for a moment, his eyes dark. Then he held out his hand. "Give me back the letter."

"What?"

"The letter," Henry repeated. "Give it back. Fuck you, if you won't help me. Fuck you." His voice cracked.

Mac reached for Henry's hand, and Henry pulled away. Just for a second, Mac wondered what he'd do. Run, maybe, like he always did. Run, and disappear somewhere Mac would never find him again.

But then Henry wilted. He dropped his hand to his side. His shoulders sagged. "Mac, I have to do this, okay?"

For just a second, Mac thought, they almost understood each other. Then he remembered that he could lose his job for knowing about Henry's stupid plan, and not reporting him. Or arresting him. And he remembered that Henry might be in actual danger here. "There has to be another way."

"Then investigate it." Henry held his gaze. "You tell me right now that you will investigate this place *properly*, and that Viola will be safe here while you do it."

"It's not my jurisdiction," Mac told him. "And you know I can't promise you that. Look, I've got enough to deal with at the moment."

Henry's mouth quirked. "Yeah, that's what I figured. Are you gonna turn me in?"

Mac glanced over Henry's shoulder at a woman and toddler who were tearing up bread to feed the birds. He thought about OPR, and about Val, and about all the shit he could get into for letting Henry do this. And then looked at Henry's face again, and caught a glimpse what might have been the real man hiding behind the mask. No, not a man. A kid. A frightened kid who just wanted to protect his sister, and who was asking for his help. In Henry's place, what would Mac do? "No, Henry, I'm not going to turn you in."

Henry swallowed. "Thank you."

Mac reached out for his hand, and this time Henry didn't pull away. Mac curled his fingers through Henry's. "For the record, I think this is stupid, I think *you're* stupid, but I'll keep your secret as long as you promise to keep me informed. And I mean that. If you find anything at all, you call me and tell me. And if I tell you to get out, you do it, okay?"

"Okay." Henry looked at their joined hands, then up at Mac. "So, do I get a code name for our little undercover op?"

"No."

"Because I was thinking, the other night, that we should make a TV show, like *The Odd Couple*, but with crime. And you'd be the one who was all uptight and tidy, and I'd be the cool, casual one." Henry drew Mac off the path toward the shade of some large trees. "And we'd have a classic car, and probably a dog sidekick. But, here's the best part. The title. Are you ready for the genius bit?"

Mac smiled despite himself. "Impress me."

"My name would be Henry Colby, or Henry Jarlsberg," Henry said, "so we'd be called—"

"Mac and Cheese." Mac shook his head. "You're an idiot."

"I'm a *genius*," Henry corrected him.

Mac's smile faded. "Why would you be called Henry though? Why not Sebastian?"

Henry's fingers tightened. "Don't push. C'mon, I was just telling you about my brilliant idea, and now you're wrecking it."

"Well," Mac said, "what's a wisecracking smart-ass character called Cheese without some secret heartbreak?" He kept his tone light.

"Yeah," Henry said quietly. "But, you know what it is, Mac? Everyone in my whole life who ever called me Sebastian fucked me over one way or another. Except Viola. She never fucked me over. I fucked her over instead."

"What happened?"

Henry turned toward him, stepping closer. He tugged his hand free from Mac's, only to reach up and curl it around his neck. His breath was hot on Mac's ear. "Don't ask me that. Don't make me lie to you."

Mac rested his hands on Henry's hips. "All you've done is lie to me."

"Not about the stuff that matters." Henry drew back for an instant, and then pressed his lips against Mac's. The kiss was soft and fleeting. "I like you, and you like me too. Don't wreck it by wanting to *know* me."

"I already know you." Mac didn't know if that was true or not. "I know what it costs you to keep your sister in this place, when you could have walked away and left her in some shitty public hospital. I know that all the lying and cheating and scheming are for her. I know... I know that your mother died of a drug overdose a year after you were arrested for prostitution. I know those things. What else is there?"

"It was my fault," Henry said. "My fault Vi got hurt. She tried to pull the guy off me. Our mom's boyfriend. My first john." He shivered. "He hit her, and she just crumpled, and then she was gone."

Mac rubbed his back. "How is that your fault?"

"Couldn't shut my fucking mouth," Henry whispered, his voice straining. "Couldn't stop from making noise."

"Okay," Mac said. He cupped Henry's face in his hands and looked into his eyes. "How it that your fault?"

"What do you want me to say?"

"I want you to tell me how it's your fault. Because I think you know it's bullshit."

"It's not!" Henry glowered. "I feel it, Mac, every fucking day!"

"How is it your fault?"

"Fuck off. Is this the Socratic method meets pop psychology?"

"Shut up," Mac said. "Answer the question."

"You can't have it both ways." Henry rolled his eyes. "You are a terrible interrogator."

"Shut up," Mac repeated, and kissed him.

Well, that worked. Henry's body softened, and he reached up to link his hands behind Mac's neck. And in that moment nothing else mattered. Henry, Sebastian, his past, his dumb plan, his criminal history or his criminal future. In that moment, he was just a guy. Just a guy who Mac *liked*, and who liked him in return.

"Okay," Mac said when he finally broke the kiss and Henry was panting against his neck. "Okay. I've got your back, okay?"

"You've got any part of me you want," Henry said.

Mac wished.

"I'll look into the place," Mac said. "And if I find anything, I'll turn it over to the local cops. In the meantime, please don't do anything stupid."

"I am totally not going to do anything stupid," Henry said, stepping away and straightening his dress.

"Says the man disguised as his twin sister."

"That's not stupid, Mac; that's genius."

"Okay, Cheese, whatever you say." Mac rolled his eyes.

Henry grinned at him, and for almost a millisecond, Mac didn't regret doing this at all.

CHAPTER EIGHT

Henry sat at the craft table in the atrium and watched Rodney Rhodes try to eat the dry macaroni. Sylvia Barot was also at their table, and she'd braided several pieces of yarn together and was humming as she methodically took the braid apart.

For some reason, only the really stereotypical psych ward patients seemed interested in craft time. The higher functioning residents were watching TV.

The place was . . . depressing.

Henry wondered if he could have been wrong about St. Albinus all of these years. Maybe it always had been a miserable place, and he just hadn't wanted to see that. But Barbara Eiling had never talked to Viola like she was a child. Had never told Viola it was a privilege to live here. How was it a fucking privilege to be so damaged you were confined to a hospital for the rest of your life? Even a hospital with an atrium and personalized name tags.

After Dr. Carlisle's lecture the night before, Henry had tried to do some wandering. He'd seen a tempting paper shredder in the copy room near the offices, but Dreama had spotted him and escorted him back to room 106, and had given him another lecture about staying put. He'd spent a lot of time under Dreama's watchful eye that evening. She was militant in her mission to bring cheer everywhere she went, and after fifteen minutes with her Henry half wished she'd put him on Crowley's morphine drip and let it flow. He did learn, however, that she loved gossip. The only time he'd gotten a break from her was when Sarah had come in with a dinner tray and whispered something to Dreama about another staff member getting pregnant with a guy named Dale Gullery, and Dreama had gotten downright giddy and suggested they go into the hall to discuss details.

"Rodney," Henry said finally. "That's gonna hurt your teeth." He glanced over at Sarah, the nurse. She was supposed to be monitoring them, but she was actually monitoring her cell phone.

"They're coming!"

"Yeah?" Henry turned back to him. "Who?"

Sylvia hummed.

"They want what I've earned," Rodney insisted.

"That's too bad." Henry put a final turquoise macaroni wheel on Mac's necklace. Then, because it wasn't hurting anyone, he indulged in a fantasy where an imaginary Mac opened a slender white jewelry box on Christmas Eve and pulled out the necklace. *"Oh, Henry. It's beautiful."* Then some real Kay Jewelers shit started happening, and Mac looked up and smiled, and the golden lights on the Christmas tree winked, and outside carolers sang under a smattering of snowflakes as Mac and Henry leaned in to kiss . . .

Rodney threw a piece of macaroni at Sylvia, and she squalled.

Mac was half-right. This wasn't a game—not when Viola's well-being was involved. But everything Henry was doing here, he did with the hope of impressing Mac. Because even when Mac acted exasperated—okay, it probably wasn't acting—Henry could tell Mac kind of admired him. And God, did Henry want Mac's attention. It was like a drug. One of the exciting drugs, like cocaine. Not Shit-Rite and Renal Eez or whatever the fuck most of these people were on here.

"I told 'em no," Rodney went on. "You got Crowley, but you ain't gonna get me."

Henry looked up. "What about Crowley?" His voice came out more Henry than Viola, but Rodney didn't seem to notice.

"It's a scare scam! 'Oh,' they tell us, 'there's not enough beds. We don't have the money we need to take care of you all properly.' Donations, they call it. Scared old Crowley so bad he signed the papers."

"What papers?" He glanced in Sarah's direction again.

"For donations! After he's gone."

"He signed money over to the hospital, you mean? Like, in a will?"

Rodney threw another piece of macaroni at Sylvia. "Chris always said, you gotta be the fastest dog on the track."

"Rodney, what happened with Crowley's money?"

"Chris was a shit-bag, but he knew greyhounds."

"Hey." He tugged gently on Rodney's sleeve. "Did Crowley change his will?"

Rodney nodded savagely. "Uh-huh! Then Carlisle comes into my room last night. Asks if I want to make a donation. And I said, *no*!"

"Rodney—"

"Chris!" Rodney bellowed. "Chris, I'll find you! You'll pay!"

He kept shouting, and a minute later a nurse came to lead him back to his room.

Fuck. Not that Rodney was necessarily a reliable source of information, but if Carlisle had approached Rodney about changing his will . . . God, Henry was close. Close to figuring this mess out, but nowhere near close to having proof.

Sarah was still texting.

He got up and headed across the reception area and down the hall leading to the offices. Peered inside the copy room. A woman was using the copier; Henry was almost lulled by the hum and click of the machine spitting out paper. As he watched through the side window, another woman came in. "You got a ways to go?" she asked.

"Yeah, unfortunately," the first woman said. "The thing's already jammed twice. Want me to call you when I'm done?"

"That'd be great."

The second woman left.

Henry headed back to the atrium. Stopped when something caught his attention on the small television mounted in one corner. He squinted at the news ticker. Somebody was dead in prison.

Henry recognized the name instantly, but he blinked and looked at it again, and again, until it rolled across the screen and disappeared.

It couldn't be.

This was something that ought to happen in a nightmare, Henry glancing up and seeing that name. A name that still had the power to fill him with so much fucking fear.

Rodney moaned across the room.

"Shhhh!"

He watched the ticker until that story flashed by again.

Jimmy Rasnick. Found dead in his cell. Police were investigating the cause.

Okay.

Okay, so who the fuck cared? Jimmy Rasnick had been out of Henry's life for a long time.

The bastard was dead.

Good.

Good—that was all Henry had to say about that.

So why was he standing here sweating like he'd just run ten miles? Sweating, but cold. So fucking cold.

Why couldn't he look away from the damn TV?

He had more important things to worry about than Jimmy Rasnick.

Isn't fair, though. He ought to have rotted for a long time. Death's too easy.

Wasn't Jimmy Rasnick who ruined your life, he reminded himself. *That was you. Your choices. Your stupidity.*

He took his seat beside Sylvia, but could barely sit still. The macaroni necklace was dumb. Mac. Macaroni. Mac was coming back today. He'd promised. So where the hell was he? And what would he say if Henry hadn't made any progress with this not-a-case?

He waited another minute, then casually pushed over Sylvia's glass of milk.

Sylvia stared at the puddle, then went back to unbraiding her yarn. Henry got up and went over to Sarah. "I spilled a drink." He pointed to the mess.

"Oh." Sarah blinked, appearing a little confused.

"Can I go get a mop?"

Last time he'd been here, Viola had spilled something, and one of the staff had given Viola keys to the maintenance closet to go get the mop herself. He didn't know if it would work now, under Carlisle's All The Residents Should Be Treated Like Dumb Animals regime, but it was worth a shot.

"Uh, yeah," Sarah said. "I'll call someone to bring one."

"I want to get it. I want to clean up my own mess."

"Go get the key from Julie, then." Sarah pointed to the front desk.

Henry went and got the key from Julie. Went to the maintenance closet near the hall leading to the offices. The closet was full of mops, brooms, and cleaning supplies. Old slabs of plywood, bottled water, a couple of flashlights, and some extra cots. Henry turned on the light and scanned the small space.

Come on...

He saw it. A fuse box on the far wall. He pushed his way past some brooms and opened the panel. Flipped the switch to the copy room. Then he did the cafeteria for good measure. He stuck a flashlight in his pocket, shut the panel, grabbed a mop, and left the closet.

Back in the atrium, he cleaned up the milk, glancing down the office hall every few minutes. The woman who'd been using the copier came out. She headed toward the front desk.

"Hey. The power's out in the copy room."

"Yeah," Julie said, "the cafeteria just called. They're out too. I don't know what's up. Maintenance is checking it out now, but I'll let them know to check the copy room too."

The woman walked away, and Henry left his mop leaning against the table beside Sylvia and followed. The woman went back to her office, and Henry slipped into the darkened copy room. He shut the door and pulled out his flashlight, then opened the paper shredder and shined the light inside. This was a long shot, but the shredder wasn't too full, and Henry poked around, looking for anything of interest.

Was surprised when he found a strip of blue paper with

ely,
Crow

on the bottom.

And *ear T* on the top.

Something from Crowley? Or was Henry just so desperate he was seeing what he wanted to see?

He looked around for other strips of blue paper. Found several more. He gathered as many as he could before he heard voices in the hall. He shut off the flashlight and wedged himself under the folding table by the copier.

No one came in.

He slipped the strips of paper he'd gathered into his pocket, and put the lid back on the shredder.

Once the voices retreated, he left the copy room. Went back to the atrium to collect his mop. Took it to the maintenance closet, and flipped the fuses on.

Then he left the closet, took the keys back to Julie, and returned to Viola's room.

"I need her to leave me alone," Mac said, slamming through the drawers of his desk, searching for his favorite pen.

Val didn't answer.

"I need her to get the fuck out of my face so I can do my job."

"And what exactly are you doing, Mac?" Val leaned against his door frame, her arms crossed.

He looked up. "What do you mean?"

"You're supposedly on leave, but you're in and out of the office, making phone calls, asking Dennis to run checks on names—"

"He told you?"

"Is there something I should know?"

He straightened. "I'm just trying to not fall too far behind."

Great, now he was lying to Val. He was helping Henry masquerade as his twin sister, he was visiting crime scenes he hadn't been invited to, he was letting a navy suit–wearing hell fiend try to destroy his reputation . . . and now he was lying to the one person who didn't make him crazy. Who trusted his judgment.

"How was your doctor's appointment?"

He blinked.

"Aha."

"Oh that," he said, a beat too late.

"Cut the shit, Mac."

He sighed. Rubbed a hand over his chin. He was gonna have to tell her sometime. "I went to check out where Lonny Harris's body was found."

"I see."

"I've gotta figure this thing out, Val. Bixler's saying this guy was her informant. This guy turns up shot through the head and the heart, and he was gonna make a complaint about me? What the fuck is going on?" He glanced back into the drawer. "And where the *fuck* is my pen?"

"Your pen?"

"Yes, my pen. My fucking pen that I always use. Has someone been in my fucking desk?"

"You want to take a breath?"

"Not really."

Val just stared at him until he took a breath.

"I don't know this guy, Val." He shoved Lonny Harris's file across the desk. "I don't know him, or any of his associates."

He had a feeling he could list them in his sleep now, though. David Halloran. Charlotte Jackson. Remy Greig. Gary Bowers. Audrey Vega. And pages and pages more. Six pages of associates in total, and not one of them made a tiny ping on Mac's radar.

"Bixler's pushing me on Henry too." He shook his head. "She wants to interview him."

"You know where he is." It wasn't a question.

"I do. Sort of. Yes."

"Then get in touch with him."

"He's a little busy at the moment."

She kept staring.

He cleared his throat. "I'm in deep shit."

"I know. But we'll sort it out."

"How?"

"I don't know yet." She entered the office and sat across from his desk. Crossed her legs. "You don't think . . ."

"What?"

"I keep coming back to Jeff. Wondering how we— How *I* missed that."

"Val."

"He worked here for five years. And he didn't— I mean, he did a good job. And now I've got to go back through every case he touched and try to figure out if he sabotaged it somehow. And it's just, like, no. I knew the guy. I would have noticed if something was up."

"Who knows when Maxfield bought him? He could've been loyal to the Bureau for years, and then last summer his wife mentioned wanting a bigger house . . ."

"I don't understand. Why put yourself through it? You've got to work like a fucking dog to get in here, and why put in the time if you're gonna throw your whole career away the day some sleazebag promises you a briefcase full of cash?"

"Dunno. Jeff was proud of the work he did here. Maybe he was even prouder of being able to play us."

"And now I've got to wonder about everyone else. Are there other signs I'm missing? People I've thought were loyal, who—"

"The thing with Jeff was a freak incident."

"What about this OPR business?" Val said. "You think it's a coincidence, them turning up at the same time Lonny Harris turns up dead? Throwing old cases in your face? Telling you Harris says you bought *coke* from him? Mac, anyone who's seen your record would know that's a lie. You've always tested clean."

"I don't know. Nobody knew Jeff was working against us. I guess they figure I could have secrets too."

"Someone's got it in for you, Mac. And if it doesn't have something to do with Rasnick's death, I'll eat my fucking sensible shoes."

"Maybe so." Yeah, this looked bad. But what could Mac do but go on living his life? He'd keep investigating the Harris thing. And he'd keep helping Henry out at St. Albinus—though God knew that was probably the worst decision he could make short of telling Janice Bixler to go fuck herself. "But let's see what happens. They've got nothing on me but the word of a dead guy."

"What I'm saying, though, is should I be looking into anyone here? What if whoever's orchestrating this Harris shit is someone close to you?"

"I don't think we've got another mole." He wanted to believe that was true. Lightning didn't strike twice and all that.

"Didn't Maxfield tell you there were bigger fish than Jeff on the payroll?"

"It was a pissing contest. He would have said anything to rile me."

Mac didn't know why he was arguing against the possibility of another mole. But he didn't want to believe it anymore than Val did. Nobody here was his friend, apart from Val—possibly Penny, although that might have been a stretch—but he didn't think they had anything to do with Lonny Harris or Janice Bixler.

But when he found out who'd told on him about the mood swings, he'd . . .

Address the issue calmly and courteously, so as not to give Janice Bixler any further reason to think he was on drugs.

Val shook her head. "I don't know, Mac. This is weird."

"Weird," he agreed. "You know a good lawyer?"

Someone knocked on the door. "Mac?" Dennis stuck his head in. "I found something on that guy."

"That's great, Dennis," Val said. "What guy?"

"Oh, uh . . ." Dennis looked back and forth between Mac and Val. "Some doctor Mac was wondering about."

Val raised her brows. "Are you really going to make me ask what's going on, Mac?"

"Trust me. You don't want to know."

"I definitely do."

Dennis slipped past Val and handed a folder to Mac. "You're after a bad one."

"Thanks, Dennis," Mac said. "I owe you one."

"I'll get you the sign-up sheet," Dennis called as he left. "You'd make a good ump."

"I'm going to read over your shoulder." Val got up and came around to Mac's side as he spread out the papers on top of poor Lonny Harris.

"Shit," he said as he read. "*Fuck.*"

"Who is this guy?" Val leaned closer to see the print.

"He's the guy whose hospital Henry's currently checked into."

"Hospital?"

He reached for the phone. "I'll explain everything in a minute. But I've got to warn Henry."

He started to dial. Realized he didn't know Henry's number. "Goddamn it."

He looked up the number for St. Albinus and called. Got the receptionist, who said she'd page Viola. Nothing happened for a few minutes. Then the line went dead.

Mac set the phone down. "I have to get ahold of Henry."

"What happened to explaining?" Val asked.

"Henry might be in trouble."

She raised a finger as though she was about to lecture him, then sighed and laid her hand on his shoulder. "Mac. Just . . . Fuck, just be careful, okay? You are this close to tripping up. *This* fucking close. They're gunning for you, Mac, and I don't fucking know why."

"Yeah." He squeezed her hand and drew a breath, ignoring the stab of pain.

Henry.

Fuck everyone and everything else. He had to warn Henry.

Henry waited until he couldn't anymore. Mac had promised he'd come back. He hadn't specified a time, but still, Henry would have expected him by now. Henry shut himself in Viola's tiny bathroom, took out his phone and Mac's card, and dialed. Mac answered on the third ring. He sounded breathless.

"Henry!"

"Mac, where the hell are you? You're not gonna believe what I've—"

"Henry, listen. I need to tell you—"

"I did an independent study during craft time today. Partially reassembled a document from the shredder." Henry couldn't make himself slow down. Mac wanted to blow him off because he thought Henry didn't have a case? Well, he'd have to listen now.

"Henry—"

"It's a letter from Crowley's son to an organization called the Terminal Patients Alliance. I don't know how Carlisle got ahold of it. The TPA handles cases of suspected involuntary euthanasia. I don't have the whole letter, But Crowley's son accused Dr. Carlisle of falsifying a death certificate. I think—"

"Henry, *listen*," Mac interrupted again. "Dennis turned up some information on your director. Seth Carlisle is an alias. Two years ago, under the name Timothy Klein, he was director during a suspicious death at a nursing home in Missouri. He was never charged with anything, but money from the alleged victim was routed into a private account. The hospital claimed it had been willed to them, but it disappeared with Klein. He is a dangerous man. I need you to get out of there immediately."

"What?" Henry didn't really care who the fuck Carlisle—Klein—was. He already knew the guy was a piece of shit. He just needed to prove it to the cops. "Mac, I'm so close. I just have to find out how Dreama's involved, and—"

"*Henry!*"

Henry had to hold the phone away from his ear a little.

"Your work there is done. We take this straight to the police, and you get out of there. Immediately."

"That's gonna be hard, Mac. It's pajama party night, and—"

"Henry, I'm serious. Get *out* of there."

"Please," Henry whispered, glancing at the bathroom door. He thought he'd heard a sound in the main room. "I can do this. You just have to trust me."

"No," Mac said firmly. "I am up to my elbows in shit right now, and I don't need you adding to it. When you leave, come straight to my office and—"

Henry hung up, frustrated. The phone started buzzing immediately, and Henry stared at it. The cops or the feds, it didn't matter—both would take weeks to get through all the red tape and investigate Carlisle, and in that time, Carlisle could easily get rid of any and all evidence that Crowley had been coerced into changing his will and then killed. The phone stopped. Then started up again. "Fuck you, Mac," Henry muttered to it, hitting Ignore. He stuffed it in his dress pocket and opened the bathroom door.

And found himself face-to-face with Dreama Carey Coleman.

Mac tried to redial Henry's cell. Twice. In each instance, it rang seven times, then stopped. Not even a voice mail. Was Mac surprised?

He waited another minute, then tried again. Nothing.

He went to get a coffee—decaf—and tried to think about Lonny Harris. What it could mean that a guy had turned up shot through the head and the heart, Rasnick style. And that the same fucking day, Janice Bixler had materialized like the Ghost of Cases Past to guide him through all the shit he'd ever screwed up. But all he could think about was Henry, who was no doubt going to do something stupid, unless Mac stopped him. And suddenly Mac wondered why the fuck he was sitting here trying to call Henry instead of going to Zionsville and stopping him.

Probably because Janice Bixler from the Office of Professional Fucking Responsibility would be on him like a ton of bricks if she found out what was going on at Zionsville. But then, what the hell did it matter? She couldn't think much worse of him. And it would be *so* satisfying to piss her off even more.

This must be how Henry feels around me.

He drummed his desk.

Stared at the clock on the far wall. It was past six. Normal people were getting home about now, taking their jackets and shoes off, and relaxing for the evening. Mac had been normal once. Before Henry.

Goddamn *Henry*.

Henry has his instructions. He knows he's supposed to leave immediately and come here. He can make his own fucking decisions and live with the consequences. He's made it twenty-five years without you. He could probably have a franchise of films produced about all the times he's escaped death and danger and then gone to bed with some gorgeous guy.

He doesn't need you.

He clenched his fists.

Yes, he does. For the moments when he's a stupid fucking kid, no artist at all, he does.

He stood and gathered his keys.

He was going to Zionsville.

"What were you doing in there, Viola?" Dreama asked. Her voice was as cheery as ever, but Henry thought he detected an edge to it. Crazy old bat. He would never understand why some people found the elderly endearing. Even Mr. Crowley, whom he'd tried to like for Vi's sake, had scared the shit out of him.

Henry moved past her to the bed. "Peeing," he said in Vi's voice.

"You were talking to someone."

"Myself."

"Oh dear. We've discussed this. If you want to seem more like a grown-up, you have to act in a way that's socially appropriate. Do grown-ups talk to themselves?"

"I had to remind myself how to do the sink."

Dreama smiled. "Next time remind yourself *quietly*."

I wish your body would quietly remind your brain that it's getting to be about time for you to cross the river Styx.

"Why did you leave craft time?" Dreama asked. "Sarah said you didn't finish your project."

He made a mental note to tell Mac about this interrogation technique—the third degree, delivered with oozy cheer by a senior citizen in a Precious Moments sweatshirt. Way scarier even than a coffee-deprived Mac.

"I was tired."

Dreama cocked her head, her face crinkling into an expression of concern that Henry didn't buy for a second. "You do look tired, sweetie. Do you think you should nap?"

I think you should get the hell out of my sister's room.

But this might be a useful opportunity. "Yeah." He yawned. "I want a nap."

"Of course you do. Lie down, now, and we'll—"

The phone went off in Henry's pocket. He and Dreama both held very still through the first couple of faint buzzes.

Fuck.

He reached into his pocket and pulled out the phone.

For fuck's fucking sake, Mac.

He thought about answering it. Trying to give Mac some signal that he was trapped in a room with the Pooh bitch from hell, and that she looked a little like she might be planning to very slowly and sweetly cook his heart and eat it.

But he could handle this. For sure. The FBI would thank him once he blew this case wide open for them. Maybe they'd even upgrade his hotel. The phone buzzed in his hand, the screen glowing.

"Viola," Dreama said softly. "Where did you get that?"

I don't know; where did you get your hideous sweatshirts and parched soul?

"My cousin Mac," he said smoothly. The phone stopped buzzing. "You're not allowed to have a cell phone unless we approve it."

Yup, mein Führer. *Noted*. "He wants to talk to me sometimes."

Dreama shook her head. "Your cousin's behavior can be very inappropriate. I wonder, Viola, what he wants to be able to talk to you *about*? Why is he showing up in your life now wanting to talk? There's no record of him visiting you before."

"Um, my mom said, when I was a kid, she said Cousin Mac wasn't allowed to come by. So maybe he got lonely? And now he wants to see me, since he wasn't allowed before?" He didn't know where he was going with this. He just needed to find a way to get Dreama Carey Coleman out of the room. And maybe a fake dark family secret was the way to go.

Dreama seemed suddenly eager, hungry for more. "Why wasn't your cousin allowed to come around?"

He shrugged. "Mom said he shouldn't be around kids."

"Did he ever do anything that made you feel uncomfortable? Like what he did last time? Touching you, or . . . or . . ."

He did his best to appear anguished. He twisted his fingers together and let his lower lip waver. "He wrote me a letter. It had dirty words in it. He—he gave it to me when he was here."

He took a seat on the bed, tucking the phone into his pocket as he did.

Dreama tugged at the front of her sweatshirt and stepped toward him. "Where is the letter?"

He looked up at her, widening his eyes. "I gave it to Mary. She said she needed to keep it to show Dr. Carlisle." He lowered his voice. "It was *really* dirty."

Dreama glanced at the door, shifting from foot to foot as though she had to go to the bathroom. "I'm going to need to see that letter. I need to know what's going on with your cousin. He could be dangerous." She stared back at him. "You go ahead and take your nap. I'll come back later."

Thank God.

She held out her hand. "The phone, please."

Shit.

"It was a present," he said, trying to imitate Viola's tone when she got stubborn.

"I need it, Viola. For your own safety."

He clutched the phone in his pocket. "I want to keep my present!"

"You don't need to keep anything that bad man gave you. Give it here, now."

"No!"

"Viola. What did you talk about earlier with Dr. Carlisle? At St. Albinus, we only have room for so many people. And we need to make sure that the people we do have here are people who respect the rules. Who appreciate the chance to live somewhere so nice, and who treat this like a home."

Oh, you bitch.

He didn't even have to try to conjure tears. They were just there. Part of him felt like he really was Viola—alone here, being manipulated by this geriatric nightmare. And part of him was still himself, helpless against his own guilt.

This is not a home.

"Do I have to leave?" he asked, voice quavering. He wiped his eyes with the heel of his hand.

Dreama sat on the bed next to him and took his free hand. "No, sweetie. Not right now. But you do have to calm down and behave." She paused, looking closely at his hand, then smiled at him.

"Is it because you don't have enough money?" Henry kept his voice soft.

Dreama's smile faltered. "What?"

"Rodney said St. Albinus didn't have enough money. He said Dr. Carlisle asked if he could have his, once he's dead."

Dreama's face froze with her lips curled slightly up. She put down his hand. "Rodney is very sick, angel. He often doesn't know what he's saying."

"Does Sebby give you enough money to take care of me?"

"I imagine so, or you wouldn't be here." Dreama's voice was stilted and strange.

Henry leaned toward her, as though sharing a secret. "We don't have as much money as Mr. Crowley. He had a *lot* of money."

"It's not polite to talk about other people's money."

He knew he was walking a dangerous line. "Mr. Crowley talked about it. He said when he died, his son could have it for his business."

"That's enough, now." Dreama stood and held out her hand again. "Give me the phone." No "please" this time. Bitch was rattled.

He pulled the phone from his pocket and held it. "I don't think that's a good idea," he whispered.

Dreama reached out suddenly, and Henry thought she was trying to grab the phone, so he jerked his hand back. Instead, she yanked off his wig. Henry froze, too startled, for a moment, to move.

"Oh. Well, well," she said softly.

Henry stood. He wasn't much taller than Dreama, but he hoped she'd feel at least a little intimidated. "Give that to me," he said, as though putting the wig back on could somehow undo what had just been done.

"Won't Dr. Carlisle be surprised!" Dreama's voice held its usual cheer, but her face looked like she'd just tried the banana pudding.

"Come on," Henry said, stepping toward her. "If I have to drop my act, you have to drop yours."

"Very well," she said, her voice low, almost a snarl. She tossed the wig into a corner. "I've been wanting to do that since you arrived here."

He stared at her. "You knew?"

"How stupid do you think I am?"

Henry was a little disappointed—might have been a crazy disguise, but he'd thought he was pulling it off well. "Always seemed to work in Shakespeare."

"Yes," Dreama said, sounding a thousand percent less cheerful. The round-eyed angels on her sweatshirt stared up at Henry in mockery. "But this is not Shakespeare, and I can tell the difference between your sister and you in a dress. And I know that man is not your cousin. Sebastian and Viola Hanes. Parents both deceased. No living relatives." She paused. "Only your sister to miss you, if something were to . . . happen."

Henry tried to take the only useful part of his panic—the adrenaline—and use it to stay even with Dreama. "You're right, he's not my cousin. That man is a federal agent. He knows exactly what I'm doing here, and if anything happens to me, he knows who to question first." He swallowed. "He's actually their foremost . . . interrogation agent." *Interrogation agent?*

Dreama laughed. "I'm curious. Is this little sting operation authorized by the Bureau?"

"Of course it is."

"And they said you could go through our director's emails without a warrant?"

How the *fuck* had she known that? Henry had checked for cameras in the hall leading to the offices.

But not in *Carlisle's office.*

Shit.

"Patriot Act," he said. Because those were two words you could shut just about anyone up with.

"Bullshit," Dreama said.

Except Dreama Carey Coleman.

"I did what was necessary to prove what I needed to prove," he said calmly.

"And did you find what you needed?" Dreama asked. Was it Henry's imagination, or did she sound a little nervous?

Henry allowed himself a slight grin. "We'll let you know."

Dreama shook her head. "No." She smiled again. "See, I don't think you work for the Bureau. Nor do I think you were authorized to do anything you've done here."

"What do you mean?"

Dreama reached into her pocket and pulled out a small silver recorder. She hit play.

Mac's voice came through: *"Mr. Crowley was sick and old, and he died."*

Then Henry: *"What? So you came all this way to tell me that you're not going to help me?"*

"I did help you. That thing where I called people and asked questions? That was helping you. But there's not a crime here. Look, if you need to do this to prove to yourself that this place is still right for your sister, then I think you're crazy . . ."

Dreama clicked the recording off.

Henry refused to let his face show anything. "Ah. You're a fan of the Patriot Act as well, I see."

"This is a monitored facility, Mr. Hanes, for the safety of the patients. That includes security cameras in the room. You're welcome to check the paperwork, if you'd like."

"I'd love to," he said. "It'd be great if we could get you and Dr. Carlisle on forging patients' signatures too."

"There's no 'we,'" Dreama said. "You're not a federal agent, Mr. Hanes. Ms. Eiling might have been willing to overlook the rumors about what you do to get your money, but I have a feeling you and I play similar games."

"I've never murdered someone to get what I want."

"Neither have I."

Henry glanced at the door. A knot of fear hardened in his gut. He looked back at Dreama. "So what happens now?"

CHAPTER NINE

Mac was almost to Zionsville. He was half-listening to the evening traffic report and half-thinking about Janice Bixler. Bixler was gonna believe some dead crack addict over him? Was gonna try to ruin his career over some bullshit complaint?

Fuck her.

And okay, maybe she did have a point about his witness. He did, in fact, know where Henry was. And he and Henry were . . . *close.*

Sometimes.

Like the other night, in Mac's house.

Like yesterday in Viola's room.

Shit, Mac shouldn't have done that.

Stupid, stupid, stupid.

How hard was it not to sleep with a witness? Especially one as obnoxious as Henry?

"No more fooling around with Henry," he said out loud.

A man in a red Escort passed on his left. Mac turned to watch him. "I'm not fooling around with Henry anymore!" he yelled out the window. The guy didn't even glance at him. Sped on by.

Shit, Mac needed to drive faster.

Just because he wasn't going to sleep with Henry didn't mean he wasn't worried about him.

Maybe Henry was fine. Maybe Mac would get there, and Henry would be telling ghost stories to the dementia patients or building a block fort in the palliative care ward. But Mac's gut told him Henry was in trouble. And Mac couldn't explain the feeling that inspired in him. A combination of courage, pride, and determination that seemed to pump strength into his bones.

It was what, at his most naïve, he'd hoped being an FBI agent would involve. Logically he'd known it wouldn't be day after day of demonstrating unparalleled courage and impressive quick thinking.

Wouldn't be all taking down bad guys and then dusting his hands off and heading back to the office to get cracking on the next case.

But some part of him had hoped—had *believed*—it would involve less paperwork.

Here was a case where there were actual bad guys, and there was very probable danger. And maybe Mac should have called the cops, but what was he supposed to say? *While my compulsively vanishing witness was impersonating his sister and investigating a completely unfounded suspicion of murder at a local hospice, I couldn't help becoming suspicious myself. So I had my colleagues look into the claim behind my superior's back while I was supposed to be on sick leave to avoid an aggressive investigation of my actions and character, and guess what? Turns out there is something to it! Now will you please go rescue my Hardy boy? He'll be the one in the baby-doll dress.*

No, he'd let Henry get them into this mess. And now Mac was going to get them out.

"I'm coming, Henry," he muttered. "Don't you worry."

Then, just for the heck of it, he tried, "I'm here, Henry. Everything's going to be all right." He softened his voice, pitched it lower, and tried again. Yeah, that sounded good.

Next he practiced lines for Carlisle. "You've murdered your last patient, Dr. Carlisle. Or should I say . . . Dr. *Klein*?"

Too sixties superhero-ish. But the Dr. Klein part was good. He'd keep that.

"So Dr. Carlisle . . . or should I say Dr. *Klein*? Maybe the court will agree that what you need is a dose of your own medicine."

Nah. Still over the top.

He pictured Henry bound in Carlisle's office, dress torn, wig askew. Carlisle looming over him.

Mac would burst in, and Carlisle would look up in surprise . . .

"Let him go, Carlisle. Or should I say . . . *Klein*?"

There it was. Perfect. As long as Henry was tied up and at Carlisle's mercy, Mac knew his lines.

Now he really, really wished he could banish the thought of Henry tied up and at someone's mercy.

At my *mercy*.

Fuck no. Not going there.

Rescue Henry. Get in, get out, let Henry thank him, then cuff Henry to that hotel bed until it was time to testify.

Shit, no. No cuffs. Jesus, was Mac seriously getting hard? Seriously?

Send someone else from the office, like Dwayne, to stand guard over Henry until it was time to testify.

No, not Dwayne. Dwayne was handsome, and what if Henry...?

Christ, what was *wrong* with him? He needed to get "sex" and "Henry" permanently unlinked in his mind.

"I'm not gonna tie Henry to my bed," he announced to the next car that passed him. "Not even a little bit."

He sped up. Why the fuck was he going the speed limit when he had a rescue to perform?

Maybe he'd been spending too much time with Henry—he'd *definitely* been spending too much time with Henry—but he was really starting to like bending the rules. "Hey, OPR, how do you like this?" he asked. "Janice? Janice Bitchler, are you listening? Do you have my car bugged? A little buggy-wuggy to see if I snort any cocaine on my way to Zionsville to be *close* to my witness? Fuck. *You.* You like this, Janice? You like me breaking the rules? Throwing away the book? Using the book's pages to wipe my hairy ass?"

Mac *was* a fucking renegade.

Yeah he was.

And it was time to *own* that sheeyit.

He turned the radio from the traffic report and searched for something inspiring.

The Bloomington Gospel Choir was singing "Nearer, My God, to Thee."

Not that kind of inspiring.

He searched another couple of minutes, and through some miracle of God, the universe, and hairy fucking manhood, he landed on the opening notes of "Eye of the Tiger."

"Yes!" he shouted, slapping the wheel. "*DUHN. Duhn duhn DUHN. Duhn duhn DUHN. Duhn duhn DUUUUHHHHHN!*"

He was going five over the speed limit. Then seven. Then ten. Then... *whoa.*

Twelve.

He was totally going to throw himself into the song when the words started, except he immediately realized he didn't know any of them. So he mumbled along until he got to the chorus, and then he sang for all he was worth. He didn't have a great voice.

Big fuckin' deal.

It wasn't his voice that was going to save Henry.

It was his entire badass renegade motherfucking *body*. A body he was gonna press against Henry's slim, smooth frame and—

Not fuck him.

That was for sure.

Wait a minute, this was Mac's fantasy. His superhero rescue fantasy. Why couldn't he save the day *and* get the girl? Or rather, get the boy who was dressed like a girl? If only for the few minutes until he got to Zionsville.

Things were sure to get complicated there, but right now, they didn't have to be.

Mac leaned back, sang/mumbled through the rest of the song, and let himself imagine *exactly* what he'd like to do with Henry Page.

Dreama had Henry backed into a corner between Viola's dresser and her bed. He clutched his phone tightly, knowing he didn't have the time to make a call, and wondering if he could really punch an old lady in the face. Yeah, he could. He probably could.

Strange, but all the old ladies he'd previously conned weren't like this at all. They weren't cold. They weren't frightening. So Henry hadn't hated their wrinkles and their turkey necks and the spots on the backs of their hands. He hadn't hated the way they smelled like hand cream and talcum and lily of the valley. But Dreama was just a fucking evil crone, and all the whimsical sweatshirts in the world couldn't change the fact that she was a dried-up husk of a human being, with only her hatred fueling her. Any second now, Henry was pretty sure, she would ask him to give in to his anger and join her on the Dark Side.

Dreama reached into her pocket and withdrew a syringe. She uncapped it.

Henry's heart raced. "Oh, fuck off."

He hated syringes. Always had. Could still remember his mother yelling at him not to touch them—he must have been about four or five—and to get the hell back into his room. And he'd screamed every time he'd had to get a shot. He hated the way the metal point pressed against his skin, pushing and pushing until something gave. Until Henry gave. Even the sight of them made his skin crawl.

"Language," Dreama chided.

"What's in that?" he asked, backing up against the wall. Yeah, he was definitely going to punch the old bitch. No fucking way was she going to get near him with that thing.

"It's just a sedative, honey," Dreama singsonged. "We give it to all our patients when they need a little help to go to sleep."

Henry glanced down at the call button hanging from Viola's bed. Dreama lunged at him, and Henry tried to get an elbow in her face. He caught the call button with his other hand, and hit it over and over again.

"Fuck off! Get off me!" She was strong for an old lady. He tried to push her away, and flinched back as the tip of the needle scraped against his forearm, leaving a bloody smear.

He dropped to the ground instead and rolled under Viola's bed. Tried to commando crawl out the other side, toward the door. Dreama grabbed his ankle.

The door swung open, and a pair of well-pressed trousers entered the room.

Not Sarah. Not even the scary orderly who looked like he could have played fullback for the Indianapolis Colts.

"What the hell is going on here?"

Shit. Dr. Seth Carlisle.

"Close the door!" Dreama said, grunting as Henry's foot caught her in the bosom. "It's the brother! It's the brother!"

Dr. Carlisle peered under the bed. "Holy shit!"

"Let me go!" Henry tried to scrabble forward. "Let me—"

Dreama jabbed the back of his calf with the syringe.

Shit shit shit.

Henry fumbled for his phone. Needed to call 911. Needed to call Mac. Needed to call anyone.

Except suddenly he was being pulled out from under the bed by Dr. Carlisle, and his phone was kicked away from him. He watched it slide away toward the corner of the room, collecting dust bunnies.

"Get up," Dr. Carlisle said, hauling him to his feet.

Whatever Dreama had injected into him, it was dissolving almost all of his bones. Dr. Carlisle flopped him onto the bed, then stood there, panting.

"Well," he said. "What the hell is this?"

"I told you, Tim," Dreama said. She retrieved the wig from the corner of the room and laid it across Henry's forehead. He swatted at it, and hit himself in the nose. "It's the brother, not Viola."

Tim? Who the fuck was Tim? Henry sighed. There were way too many people using false names in this room. Wait, was *he* Tim? He was pretty sure he'd never pick Tim as an alias because there was a boy he'd liked in middle school called Tim, but he'd turned out to be a real little asshole. The first boy who'd called Sebastian a fag. Said his name as though he had a lisp, until all the other kids copied him. *Thebathtian. Thebathtian. Thebathtian.* Well, fuck him, at least Henry didn't have red hair and freckles, right?

Wait, what was he supposed to be doing? Not thinking about Tim, probably.

Dr. Carlisle and Dreama were staring down at him.

"The resemblance is astounding," Dr. Carlisle said. He reached out and stroked one of Henry's smooth legs.

"Nuh-uh," Henry said. "No touchy-touchy!" He was saving himself for Mac. Well, not saving himself exactly. Pretty sure there wasn't much left of that particular cake except the crumbs, but he was definitely saving the crumbs for Mac. Wait. When had this turned into a cake analogy? No, that was okay. Mac liked cake. Even though he was on a diet and wasn't supposed to have any. That just probably made him like cake even more.

Mac liked Henry too. That made Henry feel all warm inside.

Or maybe that was his melting bones.

He should call Mac.

"Where . . . wh . . . wh." His tongue flopped in his mouth like a dying fish.

Eugh.

Where was Mac anyway? He was supposed to visit today. Supposed to save Henry, just like always. That made him warm inside as well.

"We can't keep him here," Dr. Carlisle said.

"What do you want me to do?" Dreama asked.

An announcement came through in the hallway outside: "Dr. Carlisle to the 200 wing, please. Dr. Carlisle, you're needed in the 200 wing."

Henry laughed. "Hey, Doctor! Y . . . yrrneeded."

Dr. Carlisle sighed.

"He knows about Crowley," Dreama said.

Fuck yeah I know! Henry tried to yell. But it came out mostly "Fffffff . . ."

"How can you be sure?"

"He just told me."

"I know." Henry tried to point a finger at Carlisle. "I see you. When you're sssssleeeping." He turned the point into a finger gun, squinted one eye, and fired at Dr. Carlisle. Then his arm flopped onto the bed. "You killed him. Thass r'lly fuckin' not cool."

"Take *care* of him," Carlisle snapped at Dreama.

That sounded nice to Henry, being taken care of. But by Mac, not by Whimsical Sweatshirt Bitch. Also, the way Dreama was looking at him, he wasn't super sure he was gonna like the kind of care she took of him.

"Where?" Dreama asked.

Carlisle glanced at the door. "Crowley's room. We can keep the body in there until after hours without anyone coming in."

The body? Ruh-roh.

"And Viola? We could say she wandered off again. And this time she didn't come back. No one will be surprised they can't get ahold of her brother."

No. No fucking way were they gonna kill him and pretend Viola had disappeared forever. No way was Henry gonna die and leave Viola alone in the world.

Carlisle nodded. "Whatever you think is best," he said brusquely. Then, his tone softer, he added, "Angel." He leaned down and kissed her.

"Ewwwwwnoooooo," Henry moaned. Maybe it would be better to die than to live with that memory.

His eyes fluttered. He needed to stay awake. For Vi.

"I'll take care of it," Dreama whispered as she and Carlisle parted.

Carlisle left. Henry opened his mouth, but his jaw and tongue went slack. "Mmmac," he finally forced out, "'ll know."

Dreama patted his shoulder. "Let's see him prove it." She stepped into the hall and came back with a wheelchair. She dragged Henry off the bed. Surprisingly strong. Henry collapsed half in and out of the chair and didn't really care. Heaviness gathered behind his eyes, and he couldn't speak as Dreama adjusted his numb limbs and wheeled him toward the door.

Stay awake, he reminded himself. But he couldn't even finish the thought before he was asleep.

CHAPTER TEN

Stacy was teaching Viola how not to be afraid. If people asked you questions, you had to make them prove they had the right to know the answers. Had to stare at them and think, *Who are you to ask?* Then keep your face straight like when you were playing poker and shrug. Or answer with a question. Turn it around on them.

"What are you doing here?" Stacy asked Viola. They were pretending Viola had been caught snooping around private property at night.

Viola kept her face straight. "Lost my way. Looking for the county road," she said.

On the floor, Remy laughed, but it was a nice laugh, not a Viola's-being-stupid laugh. Remy was pretty. Viola knew that wasn't the right word for a boy, but he was, and he also loved Sebastian, and that was nice. That was something they had in common, and with Stacy too. It was good that Sebastian had friends. Viola used to have lots of friends. Then she just had Mr. Crowley, and now he was dead. He was old and sick, but he wasn't supposed to be dead yet. Not until he made up with his son after their stupid fight, saw his new granddaughter, and took Viola for ice cream because *fuck the rules*.

Mr. Crowley had sworn *a lot*.

Stacey nodded. "And what do you say if someone at the store asks to check your bag?"

Viola knew that one. "I live at St. Albinus."

Remy laughed again. "Actually, that's perfect."

Sebastian had taught her that, because once, when they went shopping together, he put a pack of batteries in her bag because he didn't have the money for them. And said if anyone tried to stop them Viola should say where she lived. And Viola wasn't stupid. She knew they were stealing, just like they had when they were kids, and she knew that Sebastian felt bad for using her as an excuse, but nobody even asked about the batteries so it didn't matter. But Sebastian was in a bad mood for the rest of the afternoon because of it.

Sometimes he looked at Viola like he was looking at a stranger. Or looking at someone he'd met once, wondering if they remembered him. But Viola had never forgotten Sebastian.

"Viola," Remy said, "you're a natural."

Viola smiled shyly.

Remy grinned up at Stacy and batted her leg. "You think Henry would let us recruit her?"

Stacy arched her brows. "Don't even think about it."

Carson came in, threw a bag down on the table, and cut through the living room and down the hall.

"Glad to see he's in another fine mood," Stacy said.

Remy had gone still. He didn't say anything.

After a few minutes, Remy got up and went down the hall to the back lounge. Stacy sighed and dropped ash into the glass tray on the coffee table. "Remy," she whispered. "What are you doing?"

Viola glanced down the hall, and then back at Stacy. "Is Carson mean to him?"

Stacy hesitated awhile. "Rem's pretty mean to himself."

Viola understood that. Sebastian had been mean to himself after her accident. He'd ripped up his *Complete Works of Shakespeare*, and he'd broken their sled, sending it down a hill with rocks tied to it, toward a line of trees. He'd made himself stay at the hospital with Viola for hours even when he was hungry and tired; even when Viola was sleeping. He's once yelled at Viola, *"Don't you understand? You're never going to be right!"* Viola thought that counted as Sebastian being mean to himself, not to her, because really, Viola felt all right. A little confused, a little frustrated. Sometime she was angry for hours, but not at Sebby.

The door to the back lounge closed, and Stacy got up to make lunch. "You want something?"

Stacy had been letting Viola make her own food, unless it involved the stove, and then Stacy helped her. "No, thank you."

Sebastian had sent Stacy a message yesterday saying he'd be back soon. Viola was sad he hadn't called. That he hadn't wanted to talk to her.

She left Stacy and wandered down the hall. She was going to go to Jo's room and see if Jo needed help with costumes, but she ended up by the door to the back lounge, listening. Behind the door, bedsprings squeaked in a soft, rhythmic animal-whimper sound. A deep voice grunted. Every once in a while, there was a noise like a stomp, and the rattle of the TV on the stand.

She'd heard that same kind of grunting and creaking when she was sixteen and had stood outside Sebastian's door. She'd thought at first he had someone over. But the noises hadn't sounded like people having fun. They'd sounded like Sebastian in pain. And J.J.'s familiar voice muttering, "Shut up. *Shut* up."

Their mother had been asleep on the couch. Viola remembered that—slack mouth, a bubbly snore. A limp, skinny arm. A stained blanket piled on her like a dollop of garnish rather than wrapped around her.

Viola had felt so alone then, staring at the door, terrified of what was happening on the other side. She'd gone in, and her life had changed because of it.

She didn't have to open the door now. Wouldn't, because this was private. Remy had gone in after Carson. Remy was being mean to himself.

She went to Jo's room and tried on a pair of trousers and a vest. Jo said she looked good. When she left, she didn't feel like sitting with Stacy anymore, and she didn't want to nap. She wanted to know if everything was okay behind the lounge door.

So she opened it.

Carson was in an old armchair, watching TV with his pants unbuttoned. He glanced at her when she entered, then turned back to the TV. Took a swig from a half-gallon jug of fruit punch.

"Where's Remy?"

Carson didn't say anything. Then, "'Where's Remy?'" he mocked in a soft voice. In his regular voice he said, "I'm not the resident bitch wrangler."

Viola knew better than to comment on his rude words. This man said bad things, did bad things, and Viola couldn't stop him. But she didn't have to like him.

"Shut the door," Carson said.

She didn't.

Carson chuckled. It wasn't a nice sound. "So you do have some sense. Not as dumb as you play."

"I'm not dumb."

"Maybe not. But you have no idea where you are or who you're in with, do you?"

The window was open. The room was cold.

"I know you're mean to Remy."

Carson laughed. "Little faggot begs for it. And he's no angel. None of us are."

"There are bad angels," she said.

"Right now he's somewhere with a needle in his arm. That's what your little friend does when he's done playing with you."

"You hurt him."

Carson flicked the juice jug, then examined his hand. "Get on out of here, honey. I can't really deal with Nancy Drew and the Case of the Sad Druggie Faggot right now, all right?"

She knew she should leave. But Carson was interesting, even if he was dangerous. He was like all the people Sebastian warned her away from.

Except he wasn't.

The people Sebastian warned her away from usually didn't end up being bad people. They wanted to buy Viola a drink, ask her where she was from and what she did, or if she was busy this weekend. Then they realized she wasn't quite like them, and they backed off.

"I didn't like how that guy was looking at you," Sebastian would say. But Viola knew the man was only curious, or that maybe he just thought she was pretty or had a nice smile. Sebastian got the same kind of stares, sometimes.

Sebastian was more distrustful than Viola, even though she probably had more reason to be.

But Carson . . . Carson definitely wasn't someone she could trust. And she felt now those strains of rebelliousness that lingered from her old life, that sometimes flowered into something even more dangerous. Her old rebellions had been contained, careful. She had been smart enough, as a child and as a teenager, to know how far to take them. Now her impulses were wild—not only beyond her control, but unhampered by a *desire* to control them. That was why she sometimes threw things, or wandered away from St. Albinus, or yelled.

Or stayed in a room alone with Carson.

"Even your brother," Carson went on. "You think he's a nice guy? He cheats people. Takes whatever he wants from them."

"He's not like you."

Carson laughed again and stood. "Nooo. Of course not, honey. Nobody here is anything like me."

Viola stayed still as he approached.

"So why aren't I your friend?" he asked. He was so close she smelled fruit punch and cigarettes and something else bitter. His pants were still undone, but she couldn't see his privates through his underwear. Good, because she wouldn't have wanted to. "I'm the best at what I do. I could teach you to be something more than the dumb little girl everyone's made you into. Hmm?"

"I don't like you." It wasn't a nice thing to say, but she didn't know how else to explain why she and Carson couldn't be friends.

"I know," Carson said softly. He reached out like he might touch her hair, and Viola hit his arm, hard.

Carson pulled back but laughed again, very quietly.

"Yeah, I know," he repeated.

"You fuck Remy," she said. She wasn't supposed to say fuck, but she wanted to show Carson she was a grown-up. That she understood.

Carson stuck his hands in his pockets, which forced his fly further open. "Rode that little bitch's mouth just like he asked."

"You shouldn't!" she shouted, suddenly angry. She felt like she had when she'd woken in the hospital, and most of the confusion had worn off. Everything had threatened to hurt, the pain pushing against a dam of drugs. And there was anger too, indefinable and raw, because that pain had no right to try to enter her body. No right to make her so afraid.

"And why the fuck shouldn't I?" Carson shouted back, his breath hot and sudden on her face. "Who made you world police, Mary Sue? No one asked your opinion!"

She stomped on his foot. She thought he might try to hit her, and knew she'd hit him right back.

But he just grunted and bent one knee. Sucked air in through his teeth and let out a tired, almost sad groan.

Stacy was hurrying down the hall toward them. Carson left the room and pushed past her, and a minute later Viola heard the front door slam.

"Are you okay?" Stacy asked. "What'd he do?"

Viola stared down the hall. "I'm okay. I hurt him. I think." She didn't know how to explain that she didn't mean stomping on his foot. That maybe Carson had meant it when he'd said there was no one here like him, and that she should want to learn things from him. Maybe he didn't like to hurt Remy, but he did it anyway—first because it was something new, and then later because it was familiar. The same reason Sebastian took things from people. There were other ways to get money, but Sebastian had learned to understand lies and lying like no one else Viola had ever met.

And yet he always told her the truth.

Which must be a hard thing to do, once you saw how well lies worked. How beautifully and simply you could topple a whole line of facts just by creating one idea that wasn't there before.

Remy came home a little later. Viola was lying in Sebastian's room, and she went to the kitchen to see him. He was drinking water right out of the kitchen faucet, his lean body stretched over the sink. He straightened and turned off the tap.

"Vi. Hey." There was a puffy, bruised area at one corner of his lip. He seemed dazed, vacant.

"Hello." She studied him. There was a little dried blood around his lip piercing.

"I can't, um, talk right now." He was breathing funny—heavy and slow.

"I heard what you and Carson did," she told him.

His expression hardened for a second, but with his flushed skin and loud breathing, the effect didn't last. He looked mostly confused. "Oh . . ." he murmured. "Yeah. We do . . . I have to . . . but you don't need to worry about that."

"He hurts you."

"Doesn't hurt." Remy touched his mouth. "This, you mean?"

"I can clean it off."

"It's clean enough. Prob'ly just gonna go sleep."

"There's blood."

"Um . . ." Remy said. And something flickered in his eyes—a dull hope. "I'm . . . Okay." Viola wasn't sure whether he'd just told her he was okay without her help, or whether he wanted her to help him. "Could you?" he asked.

She got a clean dishcloth from the drawer and wet it with cold water. The only light came from over the sink, and she pushed Remy gently into the lit spot. He held still as she wiped the blood around his lip ring and dabbed at the swelling by his mouth. She wasn't even scared of the blood this time. Sometimes she got scared of blood, but mostly her own. Not Remy's.

He watched her as she worked, his expression less vacant, more focused, almost awed. Viola liked doing this. Had always liked when she could take care of people. After her accident, she wasn't allowed to do that anymore. Other people tried to care for her instead, but she didn't like that. Sometimes, when she saw mothers with their children, she thought that was who she was meant to be. Thought the same thing when she saw boys with their arms around their girlfriends in chilly weather. She wanted to have her arm around someone, to be part of why they felt warm.

She kept dabbing with the cloth, even though it wouldn't do anything for the bruise. Even though the blood was gone. She was watching the way Remy leaned toward her, the way he accepted her touch. The way he gazed at her like she was saving him. Like he *loved* her.

And then she realized what he was seeing, and drew back.

He was seeing Sebastian.

Viola looked so much like her brother that maybe the fantasy didn't seem so foolish to Remy right now: Sebastian was here; he cared that Remy was hurt. He loved him back, and would make him stop doing things with Carson. Would make him stop being mean to himself.

"Thank you," Remy whispered, still watching her.

"I'm not done." Viola tossed the dishcloth into a laundry basket by the stove. She put both her hands on Remy's thin shoulders. He tensed, then relaxed. "You should stay away from Carson," she said firmly. "He doesn't love you. He won't ever be nice."

Remy didn't respond, just kept searching her eyes, and she wasn't sure who he was seeing anymore.

"Come here."

She led him over to the couch. She sat on one end and he sat at the other, until she tugged his wrist so that he was lying down, his head on her lap. She stroked his hair, like she used to do for Sebby during storms. Remy's breathing quieted. He shifted, adjusting his arm underneath him, and pressed his face briefly against Viola's knee before turning it outward again.

Viola ran her hand down his neck and onto his back, feeling the tight muscles there, his sharp shoulder blades. She might never get to do this for anyone again. Sebastian felt too guilty now to ever let her comfort him—he felt like he should always be the one doing the comforting. And she wasn't allowed to have babies, because her brain would never grow up enough.

But she had this, tonight, with Remy. It didn't really matter if he wanted her to be someone else.

"Sebby wouldn't like you getting hurt," she whispered. He didn't say anything, but a minute later Viola heard his sharp, small inhale. "It's okay," she said.

"No, no, no. Vi. No. Don't look . . ." He curled halfheartedly, pulling his hands up to his face. "Don't tell him. All right? That I was like this?"

"It's okay if you're sad," she told him. Mr. Crowley hadn't liked people's bullshit. But he'd said it wasn't bullshit to cry. Viola couldn't remember what she'd been crying about the day he'd told her that. But he hadn't acted impatient with her, the way he sometimes acted when people were "bitching and moaning."

"If I could stop for anyone, it'd be him." Remy's voice broke. "I've tried."

"Sebby won't be mad if you don't. He's not mad at me, and I do things I shouldn't."

Remy dragged a fist across his nose. "He makes me want to be better. And I don't... I can't even show him that."

"It's okay." She felt embarrassed and stupid for not knowing anything else to say. She wanted to be better too. Remy's sadness was something she recognized, something she thought she'd felt before. But it was also beyond her. Not something she knew how to heal.

Remy sat up, scrubbing his eyes. "Sorry, Vi. I shouldn't be doing this to you. I'm going to bed."

"You can stay," she said tentatively.

Remy stared at the floor. Then he lay on the couch again. This time she stretched out with him. He clumsily tugged a blanket off the back and pulled it over both of them. They wedged themselves together, and Viola breathed in sweat and smoke. Something sweet and warm too. She imagined she was grown-up, healthy and whole. Imagined that Sebastian didn't have to feel guilty about what had happened to her. That Remy didn't have to worry about being better. He was already a good person. Sebastian knew that too.

None of them were bad. They just couldn't be good all the time.

And maybe that was okay.

Because *fuck the rules*.

Because Mr. Crowley said you only had to be good enough not to piss God off so completely He crossed you off the invite list.

If they couldn't be good, they could be good enough. Maybe they already were.

Viola fell asleep, matching her breathing to Remy's.

CHAPTER ELEVEN

Henry forced his eyes open. He was in a hospital room. He must have drifted off. He tried to raise his head, but it felt heavy. He looked around for Vi, hoping she wasn't lying in her tiny bed, awake and lonely. Hoping she wasn't watching him sleep and thinking he'd abandoned her to deal with her fear alone.

It took a ridiculous amount of effort to keep his chin from dropping back to his chest. No. Not a hospital room. St. Albinus. He was in a room at St. Albinus, but not Vi's room. This room was stark and smelled like bleach.

Mr. Crowley's room.

He tried to lift his arms but couldn't.

He was strapped to a wheelchair.

It all came back in pieces, through the fog in his brain: Dreama and Dr. Carlisle. Dreama stabbing him with the needle. Dr. Carlisle telling Dreama to take *care* of him. Was this taking care of him? Leaving him strapped to a wheelchair until . . . until what? He had to get out of here. Mac was right. He'd been foolish to stay. If something happened to him, Viola really wouldn't have a chance.

His hands were strapped at the wrists, so he couldn't reach the wheels. And some hysterical part of him wanted to laugh. He'd always longed to ride in a wheelchair as a kid. He'd told his mom he was going to break his leg on purpose just so he could. She'd told him not to be stupid.

But he'd turned out pretty stupid, hadn't he?

He thrust his body forward, trying to move the chair, but the brakes were on. Fuck it. He pulled against the leather wrist straps. No give. It didn't help that his muscles were still rubbery.

He rattled the chair. He even shouted a little, since fuck it, it was worth a shot. Maybe a staff member who wasn't part of the evil scheme would hear him and get him out. But no one came.

Well, not right away, anyway.

He slumped in the chair again, letting his thoughts drift. How long had Crowley known there was something off about St. Albinus? Had he had time to be afraid?

Henry didn't know whether he was afraid or not. He was too tired to decide. Maybe he'd been waiting a long time for an excuse to stop fighting. Not an excuse to get himself killed, exactly. Just an excuse to stop spending his life trying to stay one step ahead of danger.

An excuse to do what Mac promised him he could do.

Be good.

"Mac 'n' Cheeeeese," he sang to himself, his voice a slurred mumble. "Can't be beat. Delicious together..." He looked at the strap around his left wrist. "Always a... treat."

Eventually the door opened, and Henry forced his head up. Dreama stood there holding another syringe. *Great.*

She did not look cheerful. Her hair was coming uncurled, and she'd removed her sweatshirt and was wearing a turquoise old lady–style T-shirt. She meant business now.

She closed the door behind her and walked over to Henry. "We're going to do this quickly, before I get called away again."

"Do what?" Henry tried to raise his eyebrows but ended up squinting.

"You're going to take some more of this medicine."

She held up the syringe. Henry shook the chair again. "Fuck you!" he tried to yell. It was like those dreams where you needed to scream but all that came out was a croak.

Dreama put her hand over Henry's cuffed wrist and brought the needle toward his arm. "Just stay still now," she chided.

Fuck.

Henry was afraid.

Definitely, definitely afraid.

The needle was nearly touching his skin when the doorknob turned. Dreama looked up. The door was locked, but whoever was on the other side rattled the knob insistently. "You can't come in here," Dreama called.

There was a moment of silence, and then a massive thud, and the door flew open.

Mac stood in the doorway, hand on his gun.

"Wanna bet?" he asked.

Mac took in Dreama with the syringe and Henry, wigless, strapped to the chair. He didn't think; he just moved, grabbing Dreama and trying to wrench the needle away from her. She wouldn't let go, so he shoved her backward and kicked upward, catching her forearm. The syringe flew from her hand and clattered across the floor. Dreama shrieked, but the sound cut off as she hit the wall. She slumped to the ground.

Henry stared at her motionless body, his mouth slightly open.

Mac hurried to his chair and started undoing the straps.

"Mac," Henry said. "How dishoo . . . ?"

"I had to sneak in through a storeroom window," he said gruffly. He was looking forward to getting Henry out of here so he could kill him personally. Not fair to let Dreama Carey Coleman have all the fun. This was not what he had imagined when he'd thought about coming here to save Henry.

Okay, it was almost exactly what he'd imagined, right down to Henry being tied up with a supervillain looming over him. Still, he hadn't *actually* thought Henry would manage to get into this much trouble in so short a time.

"Mac? Dishoo roun'house kick an old lady?" Henry asked him as he worked on the second strap.

He glanced behind him at Dreama. She was still breathing.

"No," he said shortly. "I—I was—"

"You dihh."

"I was trying to get her to drop the needle, and she fell—"

"'Cause you kicked her."

"I'm sorry, did you want me to let her inject you with that?"

"No, Mahhh. You're th' awesomest of all the awesome. Iss juss you kicked—"

"If anyone asks, I used necessary force." *If Janice Bixler asks.*

"Fuckin' kicked an old lady. In the face. Killed her."

"I did not kick her in the face." He jerked the other strap free. "And she's not dead."

"She is *down*."

"I need you to stand up now."

"Down for the *count*."

"Henry. Focus."

Mac tried to lift him, but Henry's body was a deadweight.

"Fuckin' Mac and Cheese," Henry mumbled into Mac's shirt as Mac lifted him awkwardly and started to drag him. "Fuckin' unssstoppable."

"Work with me here."

"I dunno what they gave me." Henry's head lolled back, and he smiled. "It's pretty good though. Goooood..."

"Focus," Mac said again, and wondered if he should just dump Henry back in the chair.

Henry raised a hand and swatted him on the side of the head in what might have been intended as an affectionate gesture. "I am focus. Focusing. I am focusing." He made a strange noise in the back of his throat. "My bones've melted."

"Okay." *Shit*. He needed to call the local cops. And Val. And he needed to track down Dr. Seth Carlisle, aka Timothy Klein. And it would be much, much easier to do these things without Henry hanging around his neck like a millstone. But there was no way he was leaving him with Dreama. And no way he was not making Henry's safety his first priority. "Okay, you need to get back in the chair, and we'll get out of here."

Henry slumped into the chair, his dress riding up. Shit. He hadn't been kidding about wearing Viola's underwear. "Mac," he whispered. "Rescuin' me."

"Yeah." Warmth spread through Mac. "That's right. I'm rescuing you, Henry."

"Sebastian," Henry murmured. "You oughta rescue him too."

Mac pulled his phone out of his pocket. "Yeah? Would Sebastian let me rescue him?"

"Sebastian's *crazy* about you. He *loooves* you." Henry put a finger to his lips. "Shh. Don't tell."

Mac stilled momentarily. Forced himself to go ahead and dial the cops. Henry was drugged out of his mind. Mac couldn't trust anything he said under the best of circumstances. And yet he paused in the middle of putting in the number. Closed his eyes for just a second and placed a hand on Henry's cheek. Felt him lean into the touch.

"It's all fucked up. Isn't it, Mac?"

Mac shook his head. "No." He put the phone up to his ear. "I'm gonna get you home."

"Don't have one of those," Henry mumbled.

"You're going home with me." *And God help me, I will chain you up if it keeps you from running again.*

"Okay." Henry's eyes closed.

Mac spoke to the 911 operator, keeping a hand on Henry's shoulder to make sure he didn't fall out of the chair, and an eye on Dreama to make sure she didn't rise up screaming like a thing from a horror movie. Because if horror movies had taught Mac anything, it was that an enemy was never as down for the count as you thought it was. Mac *hated* horror movies. His sister Libby had loved that sort of shit as a kid, and thought Mac was secretly scared. He wasn't. He just didn't like unrealistic movies. Still, it was hard to shake the idea that Dreama wasn't out cold at all . . . that she was lying there in wait like some sort of swamp monster.

Mac relayed his location to the operator—as much of the situation as could be adequately explained in a few brusque sentences—and then disconnected the call and dialed Val.

"Mac? Where the hell are you?"

"Zionsville. I found Henry."

The soft clicking of keys. "What happened?"

"That's a long story," Mac said. "But someone tried to kill him. We're okay. I've got a perp down, and I've called the local PD for backup. I think Henry was right; I think they were killing patients, or at least benefiting from their deaths."

Val groaned. "When you get back to the office, I'm going to need to hear that long story, Mac. *All* of it."

"Deal." Mac slid his phone into his pocket.

"You in trouble, Mac?" Henry's eyes were open again, barely.

Mac raised his eyebrows. "Only when I'm with you."

Henry's face fell. "Uh-oh. I am a bad influence."

"You sure are."

"Did I miss the shoot-out?"

"What shoot-out?"

"Bang," Henry said, jabbing his finger into Mac's leg. "You know, when you chase the bad doctor down the hallway, and you kick down *another* door, and he tips over a filing cabinet to—to slow you down, and paper goes everywhere, but Mac, you just vault that motherfucker! Then you shoot him."

"You watch too much TV."

"Mac 'n' Cheeeeese." Henry started to hum. "Always a treeeeeat."

"Shhh."

"Right," Henry agreed solemnly. "Because of the bad guys."

"Because of the song," Mac corrected.

The residential wing was mostly empty. Mac had realized when he'd entered that the residents were at dinner. There had been a low hum of noise—voices and the scrape of chairs and cutlery—coming from the dining hall. He'd only had to avoid a single orderly on his way to Viola's room. He'd slipped inside and found it empty. He'd seen the signs of a struggle. The bed had been shifted and Henry's wig was lying on the floor. For a second he'd panicked, and then, heading back up the hallway toward the offices—he'd demand some fucking answers there—he'd heard a voice coming from behind a closed door.

"You're going to take some more of this medicine," Dreama had said. There was something in her tone that had made Mac's skin crawl. And then he'd heard another voice. Not words exactly, but a sound that was scared and angry and desperate. *Henry.*

Mac would have kicked down a hundred doors to get to him.

"It's a good song, Mac," Henry whispered.

Mac rubbed his shoulder. "It's okay, I guess."

Henry smiled, and then frowned. "So what about the shoot-out?"

"You know, after that last one at the cabin, I'm really not in the mood." He released Henry for a moment, and crossed to the door. It was still ajar, with the lock well and truly busted. He peered down the empty hallway, and then turned to face Henry. "In fact, why don't we skip that part altogether this time?"

"Awww, but you'd be awesome, and you've got to end with a shoot-out."

Mac leaned against the door, glancing at Dreama before looking back to Henry. "Is that the only option?"

Henry wrinkled his nose. "I guess we could end with a kiss instead?"

Mac grinned. "Yeah, that might work."

"Delicious together," Henry mumbled, his eyes closing again.

Mac watched Henry doze off in the chair, and waited for the local cops to arrive.

Henry awoke in a hospital bed.

It was night.

He remembered the ride in the ambulance. He remembered trying to slide off the stretcher into Mac's lap, and he remembered the annoyed paramedic strapping him down. He remembered demanding that the doctor in the ER give him his bones back, or at least arrange for a suitable transplant. He'd been adamant about not wanting the old woman's on the gurney beside his, not just because she had to be at least six hundred years old but also because he'd walk funny with a lady pelvis. He remembered Mac apologizing a lot.

The rest was hazy.

How Mac had actually been there, he didn't know. He had a vague recollection of talking to Mac back at St. Albinus, and something about a song, but everything else was a blank.

He swallowed, staring at the ceiling. He was alone. Again. Knew this feeling so well. You woke up in a hotel. Or some rich old lady's guest room. Or in a hospital. You woke up in someone's bed. You woke up, and even though you knew life could be good, even though you were willing to play the game as long as you were allowed, you were still disappointed for just a second to learn that you still existed. And were still alone. No matter who was beside you or who was calling you to breakfast or checking your pulse, you were always fucking alone.

He ought to leave. Ought to go get Viola. Find out what had happened with Dr. Carlisle and Dreama Carey Coleman. But already those two seemed like ghosts, like characters from some childhood story he couldn't quite remember. Viola was the only person who was real, who would always be real and would always matter. So he ought to find her and take her away somewhere.

Except he just lay there. Tired.

Eventually Mac came and stood in the doorway. Henry didn't know what Mac was doing there when it was clearly past visiting hours. And he didn't know how to feel when he saw him. His heart was stupidly hopeful, but there was a sadness, a kind of quiet defeat tearing at that hope. In another life, maybe this would work. Maybe Henry would be the kind of person who was allowed to hope for love, who was allowed a bursting sort of happiness when someone like Mac entered a room. But not this life.

"Hey." He tried to smile at Mac, and immediately felt his face collapse. Tears streamed, and this was stupid, this was so, so stupid, but it was such a sad thing, the way this would never work.

He willed himself to stop. He wasn't some little kid who cried when he didn't get what he wanted. He didn't fucking cry at all. Maybe he was still on whatever Dreama had given him. With any luck, that's what Mac would assume.

Mac didn't say anything. Just sat on the edge of the bed and put a hand on Henry's head as though he were going to try to draw evil spirits out. Which, come to think of it, would be helpful.

"I'm sorry," Henry whispered. It felt good to say that, and to mean it. He *was* sorry. About everything. "I'm stupid. You're right. And I probably always will be. I hurt people. All the time. But I don't know how to stop."

Mac pushed the hair back from Henry's eyes. His face was serious. It was always serious. He tried so hard to do his job right. There were people who devoted their entire lives to the pursuit of being good. And who had that kind of energy? A free fall into degeneracy was so much easier. He'd tell Mac that, as soon as he was normal again. As soon as he wasn't crying like a fucking five-year-old.

"Sebastian," Mac said.

Henry closed his eyes. It was such a stupid name. He'd known that when everyone at school had started making fun of it. But he'd still held on to a private love for it. That name was a gift from his mother—she'd given something she loved so much to him. He'd felt connected to the past, to all of history, to storms that tore people apart, to everyone who'd ever pretended to be someone they weren't. To Shakespeare scratching words onto a blank page, conjuring a whole imaginary world from scraps of the real one.

Why not let Mac have it? Maybe Mac knew what to do with Sebastian. If anyone knew, it would be Mac.

"You're good, Mac," he mumbled. "Always."

"No." Mac's voice was soft, maybe even regretful.

Henry opened his eyes. "What do you mean? 'Course you are."

"I'm in some trouble at work." Mac rubbed his head. "Bad trouble."

"You?"

"Yeah. OPR thinks I'm no good at all."

"Aw." Henry closed his eyes again. "You gotta tell 'em. You're the good guy. Tell 'em how you saved me."

"I don't think they'll be too impressed by that."

"'Cause you kicked an old lady?" He remembered that part.

"Because I was there and I wasn't supposed to be. And now I've got Zionsville on top of everything else I'm being investigated for."

"Like what?"

"Can't give you details. But someone's been spreading rumors about me. Trying to drag me down. I'm not sure why."

"Jealous," Henry said, turning his head so that he spoke into the pillow.

He was glad Mac was telling him this. Like they were friends, maybe. Or like Mac needed someone to talk to, and he no longer thought Henry was the worst candidate in the world.

"I'm gonna need you to meet with OPR. So you can tell them what happened in Altona. With the shooting," Mac added quickly. "Not—the other stuff."

Henry shifted onto his side. Drew his knees up. He wanted to burrow under the blankets. "You want me to tell too many people too much stuff."

Mac placed a hand on the back of his neck and squeezed lightly. "I'd like it if you'd help me."

"I will, Mac," he said softly. "You helped me. 'S only fair." Didn't matter what he promised Mac. Once he was thinking clearly, he'd find a way out of here. Take Viola and go.

"Thank you." A long pause. Henry wanted him to go away. Or stay all night. Mac's hand was still on his neck, and Henry could feel his heart *whump*ing against the thin mattress. "Tell me what you're thinking."

He turned his head. Forced his eyes open once more and blinked through his tears. "What do you mean?"

"Are you going to run?"

Guilt played through him. How had he known? Aside from at least four notable precedents. "I . . . It's what I do."

"But not this time." It wasn't a question, exactly, although it wasn't a statement either. "This time, you don't. You go back to that hotel room that the FBI is somehow still paying for, and you stay there."

Henry felt a weight lifted off him. It was nice, once in a while, to be told what to do. Just once in a while, though. Like this was probably his quota for the decade. But it was nice. "Do I?"

Mac nodded firmly. "And you tell me where Viola is, so I can go and get her and bring her to you."

"Oh no. No way do you walk in there, Mac. No way." He lowered his voice. "We have an FBI recruiting poster. On the dartboard. You'd just be walking into a world of hurt feelings."

"And criminal activity?"

"That too."

Mac stroked his hair. "I'm not letting you go."

"Am I under arrest?"

"No. I'm just not letting you go." Mac scowled, as though he was as surprised as Henry to find himself saying those words in a nonthreatening manner. "Can you arrange for Viola to come to you?"

"Yeah."

"Good. Do that. Because St. Albinus is currently seeking new management." Mac cupped his cheek. "And I know that you won't run if Viola's safe with you. So you look after her, and I'll look after you, okay?"

It sounded too simple, but Henry didn't have the energy to fight it at the moment. He wanted to believe that it could be a happy ending.

That, their identities sorted out and their lies unraveled, they got to hold hands and take a bow as the curtain fell. The guilty punished, the innocent rewarded, fortunes restored, and true love for everyone.

Henry wanted to believe it so much his stomach ached.

"'Or I am mad,'" he murmured, "'or else this is a dream.'"

Let fancy still my sense in Lethe steep;
If it be thus to dream, still let me sleep!

Sebastian's words.

He'd always loved that about the comedies. The certainty—the *promise*—that however crazy and tangled and confused everything got, the final scene would restore order. That when the curtain fell, it was done, and the characters were frozen there forever. No more lies, no more confusion, no more schemes and plotting. But maybe that was only true of tragedies. Maybe the only certain ending was death.

In life, dreamers woke.

"It's not a dream." A rueful smile tugged at the corners of Mac's mouth. "And we're probably both mad."

"Okay," Henry said. "I could be mad for a while."

He closed his eyes again, turning his head into the gentle pressure of Mac's hand.

Still let me sleep.

He wanted this moment to last forever.

CHAPTER TWELVE

"When they get here, you can't be here," Henry said.

At least he looked semiregretful about it. Mac picked up the room service menu from the desk. Twelve dollars for a cheeseburger? How many of those had Henry put on the FBI's tab? Shit. Eighteen for a steak burger? For eighteen dollars Mac would want to see the chef personally lasso the unlucky cow in question. He closed the menu and put it down again. "You don't want me to meet your sister?"

"I don't want you to meet her ride," Henry clarified. "My friend, she's, um, she's..."

"Like you."

Henry looked away. "Yeah."

Henry had been agitated since coming back to the hotel from the hospital. He hadn't even asked about Dreama Carey Coleman or Seth Carlisle. Just nodded when Mac had assured him they were both in the custody of the local police, and a homicide and fraud investigation had been launched. He wondered how much of it was Henry's theatrics—he liked the excitement, but his interest died the moment the action did—and how much of it was because of what he'd said at the hospital.

"I'm stupid. You're right. And I probably always will be."

He wondered if Henry had shut down all conversation about St. Albinus because he was ashamed; Mac had told him he was stupid, and Henry thought he'd proved him right by coming so close to being killed by that crazy old bitch. Except Mac didn't really think he was stupid. He thought Henry was the opposite: too clever for his own good. Which, in practice, often looked exactly the same.

Or maybe Henry remembered what he'd said in the room back in St. Albinus.

"Sebastian's crazy about you. He loooves you."

It shouldn't have warmed Mac the way it did. Not when Henry had been ninety percent Demerol at the time. And it wasn't as though Mac could ask him about it. Not when he was ninety percent bullshit the rest of the time. But he liked to think that if he peeled back enough layers of Henry, if he actually got a good look at Sebastian underneath, then maybe it would turn out to be true. Maybe Sebastian loooved him.

Henry fiddled with the hem of his shirt and didn't look up.

Mac almost missed his cockiness. Almost.

"I'll take a walk," he said. "There's a store on the corner. Do you want anything?"

"I'm good." Henry wiped his hands on his jeans. Nervous. Henry was actually nervous. "They're gonna call before they get here, so—" He broke off at the sudden knock on the door. "Shit."

"I'll get it," Mac said, since Henry seemed frozen to the spot. He crossed to the door and opened it.

Viola. There was no mistaking her. While not quite Henry-in-a-dress, not exactly, she was definitely his twin. The same warm hazel eyes. The same fine dark hair. The same beautiful smile.

"Well, shit," said the woman with her. An older woman, with short strawberry-blonde hair, and tattoos climbing her bare arms. "You must be Mac."

She stuck out her hand, and he resisted the urge to twist it behind her back and read her rights. He shook it instead. "And you are?"

"Just staying for a minute, hon." She followed Viola in.

"Sebastian!" Viola exclaimed.

"Hello, Vi." Henry hugged her. He closed his eyes tightly and buried his face in her shoulder while she smiled.

Mac's heart tugged. This was just like at the hospital, when Henry had come close to understanding what he'd risked. When he must have realized he wasn't invincible.

"Hello," Viola said, smiling at Mac over Henry's head. "I'm Viola."

"I'm Mac." He held out his hand. "It's nice to meet you, Viola."

Henry straightened and stepped away, allowing Viola to shake Mac's hand.

"Is this where I have to live now?" she asked him.

"For a little while," Mac said. He could feel Henry bristle and worried he was being patronizing. "Is that okay?"

Viola dropped his hand. "Do I get my own room or do Sebby and I have to sleep together?"

"You get the bedroom," Henry said. "I'll stay out here on the couch. It folds out, like a real bed. I'll show you your room. Come on."

Awkward moment. Mac stared at the red-haired woman and she stared back at him.

"So, I hear you got shot," she said at last.

"Yep."

"That sucks."

"Yep."

He had the impression she was evaluating him keenly. Which normally he wouldn't have cared about, except he didn't know where this woman fit into Henry's life. He didn't know if her opinion counted with Henry. Obviously she was no stranger—she'd been caring for Viola—but what if this was the Henry Page/Sebastian Hanes equivalent of meeting the parents, and nobody had told Mac?

And was it odd Mac felt somewhat flattered that Henry had talked to his friend about him? That he'd told her about Mac's injury—which he didn't think of as a badge of heroism, but . . . okay, maybe he did a little.

The woman elbowed him, just a quick nudge. "Look after him."

She walked to the bedroom and leaned against the doorframe.

"I'm out, you two," she told them.

Mac watched the shadows shift in the room as Henry came to the doorway.

"Thank you," Henry said softly to the woman.

She clapped his shoulder. "Be careful."

Henry snorted.

"I'm serious, mister. Lay low for a while." She leaned closer to him and said something Mac didn't hear.

"What?" Henry said.

"Yeah. So keep your nose out of trouble." She turned and headed for the door. Nodded at Mac.

"Bye, Stacy," Viola called. "Maybe we can play cards again soon."

"Good-bye, Viola." Stacy hesitated a moment. She seemed tired. A little unsure. Her gaze went to Mac's again. "Please." Just one word, spoken firmly and quietly.

Mac nodded. "All right."

After she was gone, Mac went to the bedroom doorway, where Henry and Viola were talking in low voices. He cleared his throat, and they both glanced up. Spooky, almost, the twin faces looking at him. "I guess I should head out too."

"Oh." Henry's mouth remained slightly open. "Um. I'll see you later, then."

"My buddy from the PD will be around soon. He'll need statements from both of you."

"The bad angel's gone." Viola stared intently at Mac.

"Yeah," he said. "You just, uh, you'll need to answer a few questions. To make sure the bad angels stay gone."

"Okay, Mac." Henry was dismissing him, he was pretty sure.

"Okay, Mac," Viola echoed. She smiled at him.

God, poor Henry. He had to know it wasn't his fault. Shit happened. Mac saw it happen every day. Was sure Henry saw it too. The randomness of it was hard. There were bad guys, sure. But mostly there were just people, and circumstances you couldn't possibly gauge your reaction to until you were in them. Sixteen was too young to start shouldering so much guilt.

"Henry." Mac cleared his throat, unsure what to say but somehow not ready to leave yet.

Henry's expression was unreadable. "Bye, Mac."

Mac left, trying not to feel any sort of ache, any regret. Whatever he might think, even if he thought he—what, *loved?*—Henry or Sebastian or both of them, Henry couldn't give him that back. Henry's loyalty was and always would be to his sister. And rightfully so. Except it wasn't just loyalty. It was a sense of duty. An attempt to repay a debt that only Henry believed existed.

Besides, Henry's friends had an FBI poster taped to their dartboard. This was hardly an advisable match.

He shook his head as he walked down the hotel hall toward the elevator. *An advisable match.* From Shakespeare to something out of one of those Regency romances his mom read.

If he was going to love someone, you'd think he'd be able to just fucking do it. What made a guy who'd taken a bullet in the line of duty so goddamn cautious when it came to something that should be fucking *simple*? A feeling. One feeling. One word. And he'd have faced a thousand mob bosses with guns before he'd sit down and ponder what that one word meant.

He almost turned back. Wasn't that what you were supposed to do? You were almost out of the building or on the plane or driving home in the rain, and then suddenly you turned around and raced back and told the other person how you felt. And then they said they loved you too, and you kissed, and the credits rolled. No word on what happened next. How you dealt with the fact that one of you belonged in a prison cell, and the other should be facilitating that.

He kept going. Even if he was going to declare his love for Henry, he couldn't do it with Viola there. Maybe he could spring it on him tomorrow, when Henry came to the office to talk to Bixler and her cronies about what happened in Altona.

Or maybe he could keep it to himself.

"But I need to know . . ." Henry wanted to choose his words carefully, then decided honesty was the best route. "I need to know you'll stay sober, and that you'll stay with her."

The hurt in Remy's expression was fleeting. "I know. I promise."

"It might be a few hours."

Remy smiled wanly. "You can stay out the whole night, you know. If you need to."

"I'll be back tonight. I have to . . . I can't be away from her that long." He glanced at the door to the bedroom. Viola was sleeping. And Henry, because he was weak, because he was selfish, was going to steal a few hours with Mac.

"I wouldn't let anything happen to her."

Henry cupped Remy's cheek. "I know you wouldn't. I know you looked after her."

Remy's smile was embarrassed this time. "She looked after me, more like."

"Good." Henry passed his thumb briefly over the swelling at the corner of Remy's mouth.

Fuck. This was so hard. There were people who needed him. And Mac needed Henry like he needed a case of full body lice; yet he was the one Henry was choosing to be with.

Henry withdrew his hand.

"Sorry," Remy whispered.

"For what?" Henry asked softly.

"You ought to be able to trust me."

"I do. Or I wouldn't go."

"You ought to be able to trust me all the way."

Henry didn't answer.

"I want to quit. Soon." Remy swallowed. "Maybe when you come back. Maybe starting tomorrow, I could get clean."

He'd heard that before. But he nodded anyway. "That would be nice. We could use some of the money we've got saved and you could go somewhere. Some of those places aren't so bad, you know?"

"Yeah." Remy looked at his hands, which were folded in his lap. "Would you visit me ever, do you think?"

"Of course I would."

"I don't think you would."

"Remy!" Henry swatted his shoulder. "I'd move in there with you."

"Don't joke. I'm not joking."

"Me either," he said. "I'll always be around for you."

Remy shifted away from him. "I'll think about it."

"It's about figuring out what works best for you. Right?"

"I don't know what would work."

"Maybe spend less time with Lonny, yeah?" Henry said.

Remy was quiet. "I know you want to think he . . . he's got something to do with it. But I do actually make my own choices. You know?"

"I know. But he does have something to do with it. Every time you start to get clean you end up out somewhere with him. And you end up using."

"Well, you'll be glad to know I've got no idea where he is now." Remy got up and walked to the bathroom. Shut the door firmly, but kept talking. Henry listened to him piss as he spoke. "Won't answer my calls. So I won't be fucking going anywhere with him."

Henry didn't answer. Remy came out a minute later, shaking the water from his hands.

"Look, I'm sorry," Henry said.

"Not your fault I'm a fuckup."

"Rem. Don't make this a bigger deal than it is. I'm trying to help."

"Well, maybe I don't need help from a criminal who quite literally hops in bed with the FBI when he needs to get his rocks off."

Henry sat there, stunned.

"No one at the Court trusts you anymore, you know. Even Stacy thinks you're nuts."

Henry tensed. Probably true. Probably fair. The others would see Henry's association with Mac as a betrayal. But he'd hoped Remy wouldn't turn on him.

Remy went on. "What are you going to do, walk into a new life and that's that? All clean, and sunny, and—and fucking *straight*?"

"Keep your voice down." Henry glanced at the door to the bedroom.

Remy lowered his voice. "You probably will too. It's probably easy for you. You can kick a whole lifetime of doing bad shit in the time it takes an FBI agent to come in your ass, while I can't even kick one stupid habit."

Remy's shoulders slumped, and Henry figured his anger was ebbing. Good, because Henry didn't want to leave him here with Viola when he was acting like this.

Henry tried to smile. "A life with Mac sure as hell wouldn't be straight."

Remy dropped his gaze and shook his head slowly. Snorted. "Idiot."

"Seriously, Remy, I'm not planning on a new life. This thing with Mac—I don't know what's going on. But it's not going to change anything."

It already had. But Henry didn't want to think about that.

"You can't fucking trust him. You can't really care about him?"

"Nah." Henry heard the lie but couldn't stop it. "He's useful, though."

"Oh, fuck off it. You like him. He's a good guy, and you've always liked good guys."

"I don't know," Henry said again. He paused. "And he's not some superhero. He's in major shit at work right now." He did, for some bizarre reason, want Remy to like Mac. And that was never gonna happen if Remy thought Mac was Super-Fed.

"What kind of shit?" Remy turned to him.

"Dunno exactly. Someone's spreading rumors about him. I wanna . . . I wanna help him. I guess that's the weird thing. He's been helping me. Now I wanna do that for him." It was strange to be talking to Remy about Mac. But Henry didn't exactly have a *Sex and the City*–style bestie he could talk about his love life with. Remy was the closest thing he had. "Might come in handy," he added quickly. "To have him on my side."

"Cute," Remy muttered. But there was something odd in his posture now. He shifted slightly away from Henry.

"What's wrong?" Henry asked.

"Nothing."

"I won't talk about him if it bothers you."

"You can talk about him," Remy said quickly. "You wanna help someone who can actually be helped. I get it."

Shit.

"You think I don't know how tough it is?" Henry asked softly.

Remy still didn't look at him.

"I'm really proud of you."

"Condescending fuck," Remy said. But there was no edge to the words.

"You can take it or leave it. But I mean it."

"Henry, shit. I'm sorry." Remy sank onto the couch beside Henry. "I don't know why I said all that."

Henry put an arm around him and rested his head against Remy's. "Because life sucks sometimes?"

"Yeah. I guess."

Something was still odd about Remy, though. He couldn't put his finger on what.

Remy stayed there a minute, then pulled out of Henry's embrace. "I'm sorry. I'm just pissed, that's all. Lonny owes me money."

"You loaned Lonny Harris money?"

"I know, and I wasn't even high. He said he had a payday coming up, and it was only a couple of hundred bucks, and now the asshole's skipped town on me."

"Be careful. Lonny's a prick. I don't trust him."

"I've known him longer than I've known you," Remy pointed out. His tone was odd. Not quite snappish, but Remy was definitely keeping something from him. He figured Remy would let it out in time.

"I know. Guess I'm just getting paranoid."

"Well, you are spending a lot of time around the fellows who staged the moon landing and burned the photos of the second gunman and all that."

Henry laughed. "You think Mac helped cover up treaties with the martians?"

"Most definitely. I think he is a martian. All the suits are."

"Should I wear one of those foil hats?"

"He's probably read all your thoughts already."

Sometimes feels like it.

Henry shifted. He was sitting on something small and sharp. He reached under him and pulled out a dried macaroni noodle. He turned it over in his hand, wondering what had become of his craft-time necklace.

He nudged Remy. Handed him the noodle.

"What's this?" Remy asked.

"For you."

"Thanks, babe. You shouldn't have." Remy took the noodle. Studied it.

"Hey," Henry said. "You see who died?"

Remy looked confused for a moment, then his jaw tightened. "Yeah. Some justice in the world, maybe."

"Wish I could have killed him myself."

"No you don't." Remy half smiled when Henry rounded on him. "You're a good guy."

Henry swallowed. He didn't want to think about what it meant to be a good guy, or to have Remy think of him that way. "Fuck off. You think I wouldn't have killed him? After what he did?"

"I think you would have. But I'm glad you didn't have to."

They stared at each other for a long moment. He could see empathy and longing in Remy's eyes, and it made him turn away.

Remy bit at one of his nails and didn't say anything else.

Henry glanced at the black bag Remy had set on the couch. "This my disguise?"

"How about your accoutrements?" Remy suggested. "You don't need any more disguises."

Henry stood and picked up the bag. There was definitely something chiffon-y in there.

"It was the best Jo and I could do on short notice."

"I'm sure I'll look gorgeous." He stepped into the bathroom. Started to shut the door, then stuck his head back out. "But if I don't—lie to me. Okay?"

Remy grinned. "Always."

He returned the grin, shut the door, and started to change.

Mac wasn't sure why they all drank at this sports bar. It wasn't even the closest one to work, and it wasn't that much different than the three you had to pass to get to this one. He thought maybe Calvin had been doing the girl behind the bar at one time, or trying to, or something. For whatever reason, O'Reilly's had become their bar.

"Hey, Mac," Dennis said, clapping him on the shoulder gently as he passed. "You coming back to work soon?"

"Yeah, tomorrow probably," Mac said. He made sure he remembered to wince theatrically. As though the whole office hadn't heard he'd been at Zionsville. "As soon as the doctor clears me, you know."

"Right," Dennis snorted. He learned over the bar. "And a beer for Mac too."

"Thanks."

Dennis raised his eyebrows. "Is Henry with you?"

"Don't you start." Mac headed over to the booth where Val was sitting.

"Mac." She fixed him with a level stare. "Ryan fucking McGuinness."

Now he winced for real. "Sorry, Val."

"Sorry?" She rolled her eyes. "Oh, you're sorry you told OPR you were on sick leave, and then turned up in an unrelated fucking investigation in Zionsville with—*surprise*—the world's most unreliable witness, Henry Page!" She stirred her drink with a dangerous intensity. "Or whatever the hell his name is. So help me God, Mac, if you're going to take sick leave to avoid OPR, which I sure as hell understand, can you at least stay home and watch internet porn like a normal person?"

"I'll bear that in mind." Mac sat. "Look, at first it was just I went looking for Henry, and then it was like this thing, you know, this crazy Scooby-Doo shit he was doing, and suddenly it was an *actual* thing, and it kind of um . . . events overtook me a little."

"A little," Val echoed. Her face softened. "Shit, Mac, you need to work on that story before they interview you again."

"I figured."

"And I need you to promise me, Mac, fucking *promise* me, that you never heard of this Lonny Harris guy before I gave you that file. Because it looks bad. Really bad."

"Jesus," Mac muttered. "I promise, Val. I had no fucking idea who the guy was, and no idea that he was putting in a complaint about me."

She shook her head. "All right." She might have been a little drunk. "You went to the crime scene. Shit like that *doesn't look good, Mac.*"

"I'm sorry. I just wanted to investigate."

"Agent McGuinness thinks he's a goddamn detective. That he's gonna slip away from the office and go interview the weird neighbor. *Bowm-bowm*!"

"What the hell was that?"

"*Law & Order.*" Val signaled for another drink.

"Seriously, does *anybody* know how to do the *Law & Order* sound?" Mac slid over as Dennis sat down beside him and gave him a beer. "Thanks."

Across the bar, Calvin and Penny were playing pool. Calvin was trying too hard like always, messing up his supposed trick shots. Penny was rolling her eyes every time. Lina, perched on a barstool, laughed at the pair of them.

"So Mac, when you're not on 'sick leave,'" Dennis said, making air quotes, "you should come along to one of my softball games. We could use a new umpire, though I bet you've got a great pitching arm too."

"Sure," Mac said, although the idea of spending his weekends sweating out in a field with Dennis and his buddies wasn't anywhere near appealing. He appreciated the gesture—the whole office knew OPR was investigating him, and here Dennis was being inclusive. He appreciated it a lot more than he would have thought. "I'll keep that in mind when I get some movement back in the shoulder."

"You do that." Dennis beamed.

"In the meantime, maybe you should actually go to some of your doctor's appointments," Val suggested.

"I will." He lifted his glass in her direction. She was teasing him, but it was more than that. They were friends, and she cared. Which was not a bad thing, given that this shit with OPR would probably drag on for a while. Just because it could. That was how they operated. He'd need people on his side.

He drank his beer, watched Calvin embarrass himself at pool, then said his farewells. He didn't want a late night, and he was fairly certain he wasn't supposed to be drinking on his meds. Just to be sure, he walked the block twice before heading for his car.

He could go back to Henry's hotel, but then he thought about how stupid that would be. Either a grand romantic gesture or a horny guy looking for a hookup . . . neither would impress Henry very much when he was spending time with Viola.

Henry. Henry was funny and reckless and sexy. But Sebastian wasn't. Sebastian had a single point of focus in his life: Viola. A part of Mac pitied him for that, for taking on that massive load of responsibility and guilt. Another part admired him immensely, even if it meant there was no room for funny, sexy Henry to come out and play. And no room for anyone else either.

He pulled his car into his driveway.

The arc of the headlights caught a figure sitting on the front steps, and for a moment Mac froze. Why the hell was there a girl sitting on his front steps, waiting for him to come home?

Recognition came a fraction of a second later.

Viola?

Why was she here? If she was here, was Henry okay? How the hell did she even find her way to Mac's?

And then, the realization: Not Viola.

Henry.

Mac turned the engine off and got out of the car.

Okay, so shit just got interesting.

CHAPTER **THIRTEEN**

Henry took a deep breath. Watched Mac get out of the car. No reaction yet.

He was wearing a black chiffon skirt and a satin silver sleeveless top, the fabric knotted at the shoulders, the tails of the knots drifting against his bare skin. Silver bracelets. Black stockings. Heels. A little makeup.

He could have sworn there was a time in the not-too-distant past when he wouldn't have cared what Mac's reaction was, just as long as it was a reaction. When he might have pulled a stunt like this just to get a rise out of Mac.

But this wasn't a stunt. This was, oddly enough, Henry showing more of himself than he'd ever shown anyone but Viola. The costumes, the disguises, the tangling of a story—this was who he was. Who he'd always been. This was what he loved.

And he didn't think he could handle a rejection.

He'd seen the way Mac looked at him when he'd been dressed as Vi at St. Albinus. Mac had been interested. He wasn't wrong about that. Couldn't be.

Mac walked up to the steps. Henry couldn't think of anything clever to say. Didn't want to be clever. Wanted to be fucked.

There was a panicked scramble of thoughts in his head. He saw Remy, Vi, his mother. Heard Viola's cry of surprise, and a thud in the dark. Saw Dreama coming at him with a needle, heard Viola tell him there was a bad angel. Saw Vi sleeping in the hotel bed, Remy's face as he promised he could be trusted to look after her.

And then there was Mac, just Mac. Taking Henry by the arms and helping him up so they stood face-to-face on the front step. Kissing him.

Mac, who hadn't been there for some of the worst shit, but who was here now.

Here, in Henry's corner.

Sebastian loved Mac. Why couldn't Henry?

He cupped the back of Mac's neck and pressed his lips more fiercely to Mac's, trying to lose himself in the collision of their breath, in the scrape of Mac's stubble, in the heat from Mac's large body. He clutched fistfuls of Mac's shirt when Mac pulled gently away, and felt a sudden terror. He was the one falling in the dark. The one who'd had everything he thought he knew knocked from his mind.

He would have to start again.

Mac just held him, guiding Henry's head against his shoulder. He leaned toward Henry's ear and whispered, "Easy. Don't try so hard."

Henry mumbled into Mac's shoulder. Not really words.

"What's that?"

Henry lifted his head slightly. Nuzzled the side of Mac's neck. "Want you," he said. "Want to fuck hard. Fast. I want to *fuck*. I want to try hard. We both need to try hard. Don't you get that? It's never going to be easy."

"Henry, Henry." Mac rubbed his neck, moving his fingers up through his hair. "I know."

Henry tried to move away, but Mac wouldn't let go. "I can't deal with this if you're gonna . . . I can't explain. So either fuck me now, or I'll leave."

He had a brief vision of himself as some mythological creature, something that came out of the water just once, for the right person, knowing it didn't belong in the human world, and then slipped back into the waves. A far more romantic notion of himself than he deserved, but it helped for a moment. It was almost an excuse for how fucking pathetic he was when it came to facing how he really felt, what he really wanted.

I want you to love *me. But that's never gonna work. So let's fuck.*

"Do you trust me?" Mac tilted Henry's chin up.

As much as I'll ever trust anybody.

He nodded.

"Can we do this my way?"

"If I like your way."

Mac smiled. "I think you will."

Henry tried to return the smile. "Pretty confident, Mac."

"I learned that from you."

He stared at the ground. Didn't want to be looking at Mac right now. Confidence. Every lie was about confidence.

Why couldn't the truth be too?

He lifted his gaze again. "I like you." Not love. The word still made Henry wince. The people he loved ended up in trouble.

Mac said, "I like you too."

Not love.

"And I trust you," Henry added.

"Come inside," Mac said.

He watched Mac jiggle the key in the door. Followed him in. Blinked when Mac flipped on the light.

Mac turned and studied him. "You look good."

That made him a little breathless. Which was stupid, because he knew he looked good. He looked more than good. He looked fuckable.

"Jesus." Mac's voice was pitched low. Almost predatory.

Henry wriggled his shoulders, letting a knot of fabric slide down his arm. Tried to make it feel as sexy as it looked. Tried not to remember that he'd learned how to move like this from watching the girls on the street when he was a teenager. From mimicking the way they swung their hips as they walked, all the way up to a stranger's car.

"How much?"

Weird, how they all sounded exactly the same in his memory. No accents, no ages, no faces. Henry pushed them away. He wasn't a whore. Not tonight. Not for Mac. He was a fucking goddess.

"Did you eat yet?"

Henry swiped his tongue over his lower lip. "Mmm. Not hungry for food."

Mac closed his fingers around his wrist. Pulled him close and kissed him again. Pressed his tongue against Henry's, and it was hot and knowing and holy-fucking-shit Mac could kiss. He moaned, clinging to Mac, feeling for the moment as though he'd really never done this before, that this identity, whoever she was, was a clean slate and a fresh start.

Mac ended the kiss and rested his forehead against Henry's. "You look..."

"Hot?" Henry whispered hopefully.

"Beautiful."

Henry closed his eyes. Grinned stupidly.

"Upstairs," Mac said, and led him toward the bedroom. Didn't let go of his hand once. Inside the bedroom they kissed again, and Mac tugged at the knot on Henry's shoulder. "Does this undo?"

Henry reached for the hem of the shirt. "Might be easier if I just—"

"Let me." Mac drew the fabric up, his eyes fixed on every inch of Henry's skin he unveiled. His face was serious, but a smile twitched at the corner of his mouth when he found the bra. "Well, this will be a challenge."

Henry faced away. He closed his eyes as Mac fiddled with the hooks. "Aw, all that trouble to give myself tits, and you don't want to play with them even for a little?"

Mac turned him back around, slipped the bra free, and pushed him down onto the bed. "I like you just fine the way you are."

Henry couldn't help himself. He rubbed his cock through his skirt, the layers of chiffon whispering. He exhaled. "You . . . you like my tits the way they are, Mac?"

Mac climbed onto the bed beside Henry. Reached up and smoothed his palm over Henry's right nipple. Then pinched it.

Henry shuddered. "Oh, shit, yeah."

"I like your tits, Henry," Mac said, and lowered his mouth over Henry's left nipple.

Oh fuck fuck fuck.

Henry arched his back, imagining that he did have tits. That he had something to push into Mac's mouth. He grabbed at the comforter and lifted one leg, hooking it around Mac. His skirt fell open and he tilted his hips, cool air finding his cock through his lace underwear. Mac bit lightly on his nipple, and he moaned, moving one hand between his legs to stroke again. The lace suddenly itched; the underwear was too small for his swelling cock.

"Mac," he whispered. "Get me out of these." He tugged feebly on the frilled edge just below his hip.

Mac raised his head. "I thought we were doing this my way?"

"I need your way to involve touching my dick."

Mac returned to sucking his nipple, but as he did, he ran a dry, cool palm up Henry's thigh and then pushed hard against his trapped balls. Henry threw his head back, letting out a long breath. Mac pushed again, fingers teasing Henry's cock. He snagged the edge of the underwear and lifted it just enough that he could brush his fingertip over Henry's cockhead. As he did, he bit his nipple.

Henry rolled his hips. He didn't speak. All the shit he'd ever said during sex— *"Fuck yeah." "Please." "More."*—was stuff he thought johns wanted to hear. Right now he *did* want to beg. He did want to swear. He wanted to fucking scream. But he also wanted to let go. Wanted to see what would happen if they did this Mac's way.

Mac slid the panties down over Henry's cock, then made a fist around his shaft. Each time he pumped, the chiffon rubbed Henry's slit, spreading moisture, making Henry clench his jaw to keep from gasping.

"I like what's under your skirt too," Mac said.

Henry tried to grin. "Everything in order?"

"I think so. I may need to take it for a test ride."

"Just make sure you give it back when you're done."

Mac stood. He tossed Henry's skirt up so that it fanned over his bare chest. Then he pulled Henry's underwear down and off, knelt on the floor, and put his head under Henry's skirt. Suddenly Henry couldn't see anything except the shape of Mac shifting under the black fabric. He felt Mac's palms on his thighs, Mac's hot breath between his legs.

"Oh God," he whispered. Mac tongued his balls, the base of his cock. Then Mac's mouth was closing around him, and Henry slammed the mattress with both fists. Felt the vibrations of Mac's chuckle travel through him, and he twisted, forcing himself to take another breath. God, he'd waited long enough for this; he didn't want it over and done in thirty seconds.

Mac stroked the skin behind Henry's balls with one finger as he sucked. "Yeah," Henry whispered. The stocking on the leg hanging over the edge of the bed started to droop. Mac lifted his mouth off Henry's cock, licked down the shaft and over his balls, and began lapping at his asshole.

The stocking fell to Henry's ankle. He jerked his hips up and down, whimpering.

Mac slid out from under the skirt and Henry groaned in frustration. Grinning, Mac tossed the skirt over Henry's stomach once more, then lifted Henry's leg onto the bed and stripped both stockings off. Henry stretched his arms above his head, gripping the headboard.

Mac leaned over to the bedside table and got lube and a condom. Henry waited, panting, as Mac ripped open the condom, and then stilled as Mac rolled it on him.

"M-Mac?"

Mac stripped quickly. He uncapped the lube and squirted some on his fingers. Then, facing away from Henry, he worked his fingers into his own ass. Henry watched, eyes wide, his heart pounding.

Mac climbed onto the bed, crawled up Henry's body, and straddled him.

Henry was breathless. "What're you doing, Mac?"

"Taking my test ride." And he reached behind himself and guided Henry's cock into his ass.

Henry tipped his head back and hissed as Mac's muscles squeezed him.

Mac was full of fucking surprises.

"How are you—?" Henry bit the question off. He reached for Mac's hips, and dug his fingers in.

How are you still single? How are you—this big, steady, reliable yet totally surprising *guy—living all alone in this house?*

For a second, Henry let himself believe the fantasy. That this was real, that he could have this every day, that this bed he was lying on was the one he could wake up in each morning, and this man riding him was *his*. The fantasy that Henry could in some way be good enough for Mac.

"Mac," he whispered, rocking into him. He traced a hand up Mac's side. Slipped it lightly over the gauze still taped to Mac's skin. He splayed his fingers against the gauze, his hand shaking. "Mac."

He wanted to tell him that this meant something. That this wasn't just Henry in a cheap disguise. He wanted to tell him that this mattered. Wanted to tell him he'd never fucked anybody who had risked his life for him. That single square of gauze taped over Mac's skin meant too much. He wanted to admit that he was suddenly, surprisingly out of his depth.

He stared up at Mac—those dark, knowing eyes hooded with pleasure—and couldn't shake the feeling that Mac knew anyhow.

Mac leaned forward. "Come on," he urged, trapping his cock between their bodies. "Come on, Henry."

Henry moaned, and reached up. Tugged that bald head down near his mouth. "Jesus. Came here to get fucked tonight."

"Me first." Mac lifted himself up again. Slammed back down.

Henry laughed, or tried to; his breath came out ragged. No way was he going to last. Not with Mac's hot, tight heat enclosing his cock. Clenching. He ran his hands along Mac's thighs, feeling the muscles that strained under his skin. All that strength. He curled the fingers of one hand around Mac's cock, working the wetness along the shaft. Thrust up into Mac at the same time he jerked his cock. The shiver ran through them both.

"Shit, Henry!"

Henry wanted it to last for hours. Wanted to watch Mac's face, that familiar frown—except this time it was there because of exertion, because of pleasure. Henry tried to lose himself in that pleasure as well, in that balancing act between pushing higher and higher without falling over the edge too soon. He wanted to make this good. Better than good. Because this was *Mac*.

"Henry." Mac's head dropped back. His neck corded. "*Sebastian*."

Henry squeezed his eyes shut. He was slick with sweat, the skirt tangled around his waist suddenly hot and itchy. He was almost there. He jerked Mac's cock faster. Needed Mac to come *now*, because he couldn't hold on much longer.

Mac said his name again. "Sebastian."

Henry shivered, his thrusts becoming erratic. Heat coiled tight in his belly, and even tighter in his balls. Every muscle in his body tensed. He stroked Mac's cock again, and Mac came with a groan, hot cum fountaining over Henry's fist. Henry came too, jerking and moaning.

The blood roared in his head as he sank back down onto the mattress. He kept his eyes closed, shifting his weight as Mac got off him.

"You want me to . . .?" he asked, his voice scratchy. Eyes still closed.

"I've got it." Mac peeled Henry's condom off and padded away.

Henry tugged his skirt back down.

What now?

Sweat slid down his temples. His makeup was probably all fucked up.

What now?

Now was the time he got up, gathered his clothes, and got the fuck out. Shoved his money in his pocket and didn't make eye contact, because you never knew how a trick would react to that. Dirty little faggot whore, looking him in the eye.

This was a mistake. He'd wanted it, he'd needed it, but it was a mistake all the same. Mac's fault too. Bringing Sebastian into this and reminding him exactly who he was. How fucking vulnerable he was. Shit, even Henry hated to look Sebastian in the face.

Dirty little faggot whore.

He'd come here to do something good, but there was nothing he touched that didn't go to shit.

The mattress dipped beside him. "Henry?"

He forced his eyes open. "Yeah?"

Mac loomed over him, and for a moment Henry's heart faltered. Then Mac kissed him gently. "Are you staying the night?"

That's not a good idea.

"Do you want me to?"

"Yes."

No hesitation. No bullshit. Just *yes*.

The knot of unease in Henry's gut loosened. "I can stay a few hours, but then I have to get back to Vi."

"Okay." Mac smoothed Henry's hair back. "So, do you want to eat?"

"No." Henry reached out and linked his fingers through Mac's. "Maybe I just want to lie here and make out for a while."

Mac grinned. "That could work too."

"You don't need to drive me," Henry said. "I can get a taxi."

"I'll drive you."

"Thanks." Henry didn't look him in the eye.

Mac wondered what the hell had happened to the guy who'd showed up at his house in drag. The guy who'd gone undercover at St. Albinus. The guy with a dumb plan, a reckless grin, and no fear. Something had changed. In the bedroom, somewhere between Henry and Sebastian, something had changed. He felt like he'd lost Henry, and Sebastian was still out of his reach. Still hiding in the shadows. Mac didn't know how to draw him into the open. A part of him wondered if he wanted to. Who the hell was Sebastian Hanes anyway? Apart from the best sex he'd had in longer than he could remember.

Of course it was, that sour voice in the back of Mac's head told him. He's a *professional*.

He watched Henry adjust the silver top so that it hid the straps of his bra. Mac dressed too, pulling on jeans and a sweatshirt and feeling as though every piece of clothing he added was as solid and impenetrable as armor. That whatever closeness they'd had was gone now.

"Henry," he said at last. "Will you look at me?"

Henry turned. His brilliant smile wavered a little at the edges. "Sure, Mac."

Mac sat down heavily on the end of the bed. He took Henry's hand and drew him near. Widened his legs to bring Henry close. "Is something wrong?"

"No," Henry lied. Very obviously lied. "Mac and Cheese. Perfect together, remember?"

"I remember." He searched Henry's face. "Look, I don't want to do the whole awkward postsex talk, but me and you, are we okay?"

"Sure."

Mac frowned up at him. "Henry, c'mon, don't bullshit me."

Henry put his arms around Mac's neck and leaned down to kiss him on the head. "We're okay. We're peachy."

"I don't want what just happened to . . . to ruin what we had."

Henry drew back. "Mac, please. This isn't a teen movie. Sex doesn't ruin anything. Sex makes everything *better*. You wanted it, and I wanted it, and I came so hard I'm pretty sure I blew a few blood vessels. It was *fun*."

"Fun," Mac said cautiously.

Henry rubbed against him. "Yeah. Fun. You know how to have fun, right, Mac?"

Henry had recovered, and Sebastian had retreated back behind the walls that Henry had built for him. And apparently they were going to pretend that every bit of vulnerability he'd shown to Mac had never happened, or was nothing more than part of the game. Mac wondered if that was why he'd dressed as a woman, really. To give himself permission to be vulnerable, just for a little while. Or to at least have something to blame it on if it happened. Because he hadn't come dressed as a femme fatale or a cold seductress whose unapologetic sexuality was her weapon of choice. He'd come dressed like an ordinary girl on a date. He'd been nervous.

Mac forced a smile. "Of course I do."

"Yeah." Henry stepped back. "I'd say you do."

Mac drove him to the hotel. Henry stared out the window the whole time. Seemed like ages ago, their first drive together from Dayton to the Indianapolis field office. And Henry had chatted the whole way, seizing every opportunity to antagonize him. Mac had thought, *What a privileged little shit. What a stupid kid. Clever, yeah—too clever for his own good. But stupid. Convinced that cheating people was a game.*

Mac's job was to read people. To think like a criminal. To understand why people did the shitty things they did. So how had he missed so much about Henry? The sadness, the fear? The loneliness? It wasn't just cockiness, which was what he'd seen in Henry at first. If Henry didn't believe in himself, in his ability to lie, to manipulate, to get what he needed—then Viola was in trouble. Henry had to believe his own illusion. *Had* to. There was no other option.

Unless . . .

Unless what? Unless Mac gave him money? Dusted him off and said, *Use this for good only*, and sent Henry into a new, reformed life?

Unless Mac said, *Move in with me*, and Henry threw his arms around him and said, *Oh, Mac, yes, a thousand times yes!*

And what, Viola would move in too? Live in the spare room, and Henry and Mac would care for her together?

He snorted.

"What?" Henry glanced over at him.

He shook his head. "It's nothing."

When they pulled up at the hotel, he left the car running and got out when Henry did. They stood on the sidewalk together. Mac couldn't think of anything to say, so he opened his mouth to remind Henry to come to the office in the morning for the OPR interview. But he couldn't say it, because Henry was looking at him with an expression he didn't understand; that he worried he was misinterpreting in the dark, because it looked like fear, but more than that. Fear and . . . what? Resolve?

Henry surprised him by stepping forward and putting his arms around him. He rested his head against Mac's shoulder and let out a breath that passed through the fabric of his shirt, warming his skin. "I don't want to run anymore," he said softly.

Mac brought his arms up and tightened them around Henry. Wanted to close his eyes, but kept them open and looked at the lights of the city. He set his chin on Henry's dark hair. "You don't have to."

Henry tensed. "Gonna have to someday."

"No. There are other ways."

"You know 'em? I'm all ears."

Mac sighed, and strands of Henry's hair fluttered. "There's time to figure it out. You hear me? We have time."

"How much?" Henry sounded young.

"I don't know. But we'll figure it out." Must have seemed like an empty promise to Henry, but it wasn't empty. Mac meant it with everything in him. He just wasn't sure exactly how to deliver. He was in this now, for good. Standing there with Henry surrendering to him, he knew he couldn't walk away even if he wanted to.

"We?"

"Yep."

Henry tried to step back, but Mac wouldn't let him. Henry looked up. "Fuck, Mac, I don't want you to . . . to . . ."

"To what?"

"To give up . . . whatever you'd have to give up."

"What would I have to give up?"

"You've got a job you love where you do good things for people. You can't... There's no room for me. I'd spoil your reputation."

"Enough."

"I know you're—you were probably lonely. I get that. Me too. I think that's why we—why we're here now." Henry stumbled every few words. "We were both... We *are* both... But, um, we'll both lose. If we go any further. Don't you think?"

Mac took him by the shoulders. "That's not what I think."

"You want to do good things," Henry went on, his eyes searching Mac's. "That's why you want to know about Sebastian. You think you can fix me or something, but it's not going to work. I'll always be who I am. And who I am won't work with who you are."

"Says who?"

Henry gave a small, bitter laugh and dipped his head.

"Mac and Cheese go great together."

Henry shook his head, staring at the ground now. "It's not a very natural food, you know? Someone had to think to put reeking, fermented milk on top of pasta."

"Well, it wasn't a half-bad idea, you have to admit."

"It's processed. It's manufactured." Henry looked up again. "It's fake."

Mac wanted to make a joke. Something about how he liked orange cheese. But he couldn't just brush off Henry's fears like that. Henry was giving him something honest here. So all he said, softly, was, "Stay."

It wasn't enough.

Henry stepped back. "I'll see you around."

Then he turned, his skirt flying on the breeze, and vanished into the hotel.

CHAPTER **FOURTEEN**

Remy was asleep on the folded-out couch when Henry got back to the room.

He checked on Viola.

She was awake, leafing through a book on garden birds. "Where'd you get that?" he asked, sitting on the bed beside her.

"Remy gave it to me."

That was Remy. Picking up random stuff at garage sales and secondhand shops. Not just items he might dress up and resell for far more than they were worth, but books and costume pieces. Maps. Knickknacks he'd keep until the day he got desperate enough to sell them for drug money. "Those are nice pictures."

Viola nodded. The one she was looking at was a black and yellow bird with a large, blunt beak. "Evening Grosbeak," the caption said.

"I'm gonna go to bed now," Henry said. "Are you gonna get some sleep? It's late."

"I can stay on my own." She studied the page intently. "You didn't have to leave Remy with me."

"You like Remy."

"I know. But I can stay on my own."

"That wouldn't be safe."

"I used to stay on my own," Viola said, scowling up at him.

Shit. He didn't want to turn this into a thing, but experience told him that's where it was headed. Sometimes Viola got stubborn when she was told what to do, and sometimes that stubbornness transformed into a full-blown tantrum. He wasn't sure he could deal with that today.

"I know you did." He lowered his voice. "I know you can look after yourself. But it was good you were here to look after Remy too, okay?"

Viola's face lit up. "I can look after Remy!"

Henry forced a smile. "You did a good job. He's sleeping soundly."

"I did." Viola closed the book. "I didn't let him hurt himself again."

Henry's stomach twisted. "Hurt himself?"

"With Carson." Viola frowned once more. "He *fucks* Carson, even though Carson is mean to him."

God. A few days in the Court of Miracles and even Viola knew what was going on.

"That's a bad word," Viola said, dropping her voice to a whisper, "but it's true."

"I know it is." Henry laid his hand over hers. "Remy . . . He's . . . he's . . ." He had no idea how to even begin to explain the cycle of addiction to Viola.

"He's like Mom," Viola said.

Shit. Henry hated it when he underestimated her. Of course she knew addiction. They'd both lived it, every day for years, with their mother.

Viola pulled her hand away. "He's unhappy."

"Yeah, Remy's unhappy."

"So is Carson," she said solemnly.

Henry made a face.

"Do you have to go away again?"

"Not yet. Now I just want to go to bed. Maybe tomorrow we can go to the museum or something."

"Okay." Her attention was caught by the book again.

He squeezed her shoulder and got up. Turned. "I'll be in the other room with Remy. You can call me if anything's wrong."

"I know." She waved at him without looking up from the bird book.

"Good night, Vi."

"Bye, Sebby."

"Not good-bye," he told her. "Good night."

She didn't answer.

He closed the door quietly, and headed for the bathroom. He showered and pulled on a pair of track pants. Checked himself out in the mirror, marveling at the change. His lean, flat chest and the muscles cording in his arms as he leaned on the sink. No trace of femininity in him now. He'd discarded it on the floor in his bundle of women's clothes.

He returned to the main room and climbed into bed with Remy.

"Hey," Remy mumbled as the bedsprings shifted. "Vi's asleep?"

"She's reading your book."

Remy blinked at him. "You have a good night?"

"Yeah."

"You want me to go?"

"You can stay if you want."

"Okay." Remy yawned. "Henry?"

"Yeah?"

"Your fed's okay?" There was that odd tone again. Henry wished he knew what the fuck was going on in Remy's head.

"What do you mean?"

"Mac? He's okay?"

Henry allowed himself a grin as he tucked Remy's body closer to his. "Better than okay."

Remy was tense.

"What's wrong?" Henry asked.

"I don't... I dunno." He was silent for a moment. "Gonna... Was thinking about rehab. Gonna get clean, Henry. Get better for you."

Henry swallowed.

For you.

Wasn't that what he'd almost said to Mac tonight? It's what he'd meant. And maybe why he hadn't believed it. He was just as fucked up as Remy, wasn't he? Just as much an addict in his own way. Just as hopeless.

"Okay," he murmured, fighting to keep his voice steady. "Love you, Remy."

"Love you too." Remy smiled, already dozing again.

Henry lay awake and stared at the ceiling.

Some relationships just didn't work. People like Henry, people like Remy, they lied, they manipulated. It was twisted into the strands of their DNA. They didn't get better. Good people didn't raise them up. They dragged good people down.

Which should have meant that Henry and Remy were perfect for each other, shouldn't it? Except they weren't. In moments like these, the quiet, peaceful moments, they were perfect. But these moments didn't last. They shattered with the dawn, always.

He closed his eyes and tried to imagine the fantasy: Remy clean, and Henry going straight. He and Mac together, for real.

It came from the same part of him where his mom was still alive, and like she'd been in the good times. Where there was no constant parade of dealers and boyfriends, who were often the same guy, in her life. Where there was no J.J. Where Viola hadn't been hurt. Where she was as clever and vibrant and healthy as she'd always been. A fantasy where Sebastian was happy too. It was a fantasy where there was no Henry at all, because there had never been any need for him.

He fell into an uneasy sleep and woke with Remy sitting beside him, staring at the wall and twisting the blanket.

"Rem? You okay?"

When Remy didn't answer, Henry sat up and swung his legs over the side of the bed.

"Where are you going?"

Henry rubbed his eyes. "Nowhere. Just, uh . . ." He yawned. "You're up early."

Remy gazed at Henry for several seconds, and he felt Remy's pain like it was his own. Henry had never been in unrequited love before, but he imagined it sucked.

"I have to tell you something," Remy whispered.

His tone made Henry uneasy. "Yeah?"

"Um . . ." Remy fussed with the blanket, which was piled around his slim body. His nails were bitten to red jagged slivers. They hadn't been like that when Henry had left him last night. "I didn't want to say anything. I thought it was nothing. But then you said . . ." He stopped.

"Rem?"

"Last night you said Mac was in some shit at work." Remy paused again. He pulled on a thread at the edge of the blanket until it unraveled partway. "And I thought you should know Lonny . . . Lonny told me he was getting paid to help bring down a fed."

"What?" Shock too huge and cold to register at first. Then it piled into Henry, and he stood so fast his vision went shadowy. "Lonny was gonna bring down an agent? How? Who bought him?"

"I don't know! I swear, Henry, I don't know. He didn't say much. He was nervous, didn't trust the guys he was dealing with. And now I'm thinking . . . What if something happened?"

"Remy, what the *fuck*? You think the fed was Mac?"

"I didn't think so until you said something."

"Why the *hell* didn't you tell me last night?"

"I didn't— I don't know for sure," Remy pleaded. "And I don't— You know I don't think it's a good idea, you being involved with the FBI."

Henry didn't trust himself to get any closer to Remy without lashing out. It was irrational, he knew, because in Remy's place, he might have done the same thing. But last night—Remy had had this information *last night*, when Henry had told him Mac was in trouble. And he'd kept it from him.

"Jesus *Christ*," Henry muttered, grabbing his phone. He dialed Mac's number. No answer. He dialed again. Voice mail. "Mac. Call me," he said to the machine.

Motherfucker.

He rounded on Remy.

"Can I trust you to do *something* for me?" He couldn't fucking think straight. What if Mac had already been arrested? Who knew what damage Lonny Harris had managed?

"I don't wanna get involved." The hardness in Remy's tone didn't do much to cover his fear.

"I'm not asking you to. I'm asking you to stay here with Vi while I go to the office and find Mac. Can you do that much for me?"

Remy stared at him a moment, then nodded.

"Just stay the fuck here until I get back."

"All right," Remy said. "But then I'm outta here, Henry."

"Fine," Henry said coldly.

Remy sighed and leaned back against the headboard. "I knew you'd be pissed."

"Yeah, well." Henry pulled on his clothes. "Then you should have told me last night."

"I didn't have to tell you at all!"

Henry ignored that. Stalked across the room and peered into the bedroom. Viola was asleep, a half smile on her face as though she was dreaming of something wonderful. He wondered what her dreams were like now, and if they were ever the same as his own. But maybe Vi didn't remember what had happened. Maybe she didn't see it over and over again, or hear the awful sound of her head cracking against the floor.

Her heart had stopped on the way to the hospital. Henry's had as well, and it felt as though it had never beat the same again.

And now, for the first time in his life, he wanted to protect someone besides his sister. He wanted to let someone new in.

He didn't have a future with Mac. But he had right now.

And right now, Mac needed his help.

Mac lay in bed, drifting in that pleasant place between asleep and awake.

His bed smelled of the perfume Henry had worn, and sweat, and . . . other things. It had been a long time since he had needed to change the sheets for that reason. And while it was nice that he'd finally broken his dry spell, and broken it with Henry, of course it had been a mistake as well.

Mac groaned.

Yep, here came regret, right on cue.

Because Henry was a criminal. He was also a witness. The rules still applied, or should have. It was just so damned easy to ignore them when it came to Henry Page and all of his incarnations. Even with OPR breathing down his neck, it was still too damned easy.

Mac rubbed the gauze over his wound. He'd definitely overdone it last night. He hoped he hadn't pulled any stitches. He should probably swing by his doctor's office before going into work.

Work.

His eyes flashed open and he turned his head to check his alarm clock. Which he hadn't set last night. It was ten past nine. Shit. It was ten past nine . . . and fuck it, he was on sick leave, wasn't he? Except he wanted to be at the office when OPR spoke to Henry. Mostly to see the looks on their faces when they came out of the interview room after trying to get a straight answer out of Henry Page.

And, of course, to make sure Henry actually showed up.

Mac climbed out of bed and headed for the bathroom. He fumbled with the plastic bag and duct tape system he'd come up with to keep his gauze dry, then stepped under the shower. Took the soap and washed off all traces of Henry, a little regretful as the suds swirled around his feet.

Henry Page.

Sebastian Hanes.

Whatever he called himself, Mac still wanted him. He was like sugar, like cake. One taste didn't kill the craving at all, however unhealthy you knew it was. No, just one little taste, and you wanted the whole thing.

He turned the shower off. He reached for his towel, dried himself, then peeled the plastic off his gauze. The tape pulled at his skin.

He returned to his bedroom.

He wasn't worried about what Henry would tell OPR.

What happened at Altona was completely aboveboard. Mac had shot and killed the man who'd come to shoot Henry. He'd been protecting a witness, as simple as that. Shit. He hoped Henry didn't mention the impromptu Shakespeare performance beforehand. And the discussion about spanking.

He wouldn't, he tried to reassure himself. Even Henry knew where the line was. Mostly.

Henry would back him.

It was Lonny Harris that Mac worried about. Shame the guy was dead. If he hadn't been, Mac would have been asking him some pretty hard questions. Like why the fuck he was trying to ruin his life. And who had put him up to it.

Jimmy fucking Rasnick.

Well, not actually Jimmy. But the fact Lonny had been shot in Jimmy's signature style couldn't have been a coincidence.

THIS IS ON YOU, PIG.

It wasn't rocket science. He was being set up because of Jimmy Rasnick. So why the hell couldn't OPR dig a little deeper and see that?

Because someone had handed Mac to them on a platter, and they couldn't see any further than the hard-on they got from the chance to bring him down.

Janice Bixler had suggested he get a lawyer.

He would. Some fast-talking hotshot asshole who'd run rings around OPR. And then Mac would demand a written apology so that he could print it out, roll it up, and shove it up Bixler's ass.

Fucking bitch.

This wasn't a fight Mac was going to lose.

Eye of the tiger and all that.

He headed downstairs to grab some breakfast before going in to work.

Henry didn't even bother with the elevator when he got to the field office. He took the stairs to the fifth floor and did some on-the-go reflecting that the last time he'd been in this stairwell, he'd been making an escape. And here he was, *willingly* going into this den of rules and regulations and men with the same exact haircut.

He was glad Mac was bald.

It showed style.

He burst onto Mac's floor and would have run straight for his office, except that two women were standing directly in his path. Their faces were so close to each other that they were either about to make out, or rip out each other's throats. One was Val. The other was a woman he'd never seen before. She had dark hair in a low ponytail and wore a navy suit.

Everyone was watching the confrontation from their cubicles. Penny had her hand frozen inside a giant bag of M&M's.

"If he's not here, that's hardly my fault," Val said tightly to the other woman. "He's on leave."

"On leave?" Navy Suit raised her brows. "Funny, I have it on good authority he's spent most of his 'sick leave' in Zionsville."

Shit. Henry quickly stepped into the alcove where the restrooms were.

"I'm not in the habit of tracking the movements of my agents when they're on leave."

"If you're protecting him," Navy Suit shot back, "I promise you, I will have you arrested too."

"If you think you have any shot at making your charges against Mac stick—"

"I have reason to believe Agent McGuinness has conducted himself inappropriately with his witness."

Val fell silent. Henry pressed closer to the wall.

Depended on your definition of inappropriate.

And charges? This must be OPR. What were they going to charge Mac with? Being too sexy for his shirt, pants, and boxers?

"You're out of your mind." Val's tone was cold.

Navy Suit had to tilt her chin up to keep eye contact, since Val was about a foot taller, and yes, Henry decided, it definitely looked like they were going to make out. Except that Val's expression was terrifying.

So it looked like they were going to make out, but then Val was going to suck the short bitch's soul out through her mouth.

"We found cocaine," Navy Suit went on smugly, "*in his office.*"

Henry actually laughed. Cocaine? Mac didn't even let himself have donuts.

Except that one time.

Crazy OPR lady didn't seem to hear him, but Val's gaze definitely flicked to the alcove. Oops.

But a second later, Val's attention was on Crazypants again. "Yes, because Mac would keep his cocaine in his desk next to the stapler."

As if on cue, two guys in navy suits walked out of Mac's office holding two small bags. The "evidence," Henry supposed.

"Agent Kimura," Navy Suit said, "I understand you are *close* with Agent McGuinness, but this looks very bad for him. I suggest—"

"What this looks like," Val interrupted, "is a farce. Anyone can see it's a setup. Ms. Bixler, I really don't have time for this."

There was no trace of a smile on Ms. Bixler's face. "I'd be careful, *Agent* Kimura. I don't think you know what you're dealing with." Bixler stepped back. "We're going to pay a visit to Agent McGuinness's home. If he's not there—and if he remains absent for any significant length of time, I'll be back here with a pair of handcuffs for you." She looked at the two navy suit guys. "Come on."

The trio headed for the elevator. Henry sort of wished they'd all simultaneously put on sunglasses first.

He was so busy watching them go he didn't realize Val was beside him until she said, in a low voice, "Can you get there first?"

He whirled. "Huh?"

"To Mac's place. Can you get there before they do?"

Henry stared at her.

"Henry, are you conscious?" Val snapped.

"Uh, yeah. I can get there first." Was she asking him to . . . ?

Suddenly Penny was there too, and she was handing him a key. "Take my car. The black Honda, first floor of the garage. Third space on your right. I'll wait as long as I can before reporting it stolen."

"What should I . . . I mean, where should I . . . ?" He'd arrived here in full hero mode, ready to warn Mac he was in danger and spirit him away if necessary. But with two law enforcement officials staring at him, he felt decidedly nervous. He wasn't sure he was understanding them correctly. It didn't make sense to find himself on the same page as the FBI.

He wondered if this was one of the signs of the Apocalypse.

"Take him somewhere safe," Val said. "He needs to stay away from Indianapolis."

"Okay." Henry frowned. "I, um, I've got my . . . my sister at the hotel. I'll have to take him back there for just a minute."

"That's fine, whatever." Val waved him off. "Just *go*."

That's fine, whatever?

Things sure had changed at the Indianapolis field office since he was last here.

Something clicked in his mind, and he remembered why he'd come in the first place. "Val," he said. "It's Lonny Harris. Someone's paying him to bring Mac down. I can't prove it yet, but I know a guy who—"

"I know," Val said. "I figured it was something like that. We'll get it sorted out, but now, you need to get Mac. Got it, Henry? I'm telling you to run."

He nodded. "Okay. Okay." Why was he still nodding? "You can trust me."

Dumbest thing he could have said. She couldn't trust him. No one could.

But to his surprise, Val said, "I know," and headed back toward her office.

So Henry ran.

With the FBI's full permission and Penny's bag of M&M's for the road.

CHAPTER **FIFTEEN**

Mac was almost out the door when someone knocked on it. He opened it to Henry.

"You need to get out of here, Mac."

"Huh?"

Henry stepped inside and shut the door. He looked jittery, and his left palm was stained rainbow colors. "OPR's on their way. They've got a warrant for your arrest. We need to run."

"My *arrest*?"

"They found coke in your office. Not the refreshing beverage."

"What the fuck?" Mac was stunned. "I do *not* have—"

"No shit, Mac, but the longer you stand there shouting, the better the chances you'll be apprehended by the Bixler Brigade. Now come on."

"How would you know ab—"

"I was there! I went to the fucking office to find you."

"Why?" Something wasn't right. The Henry standing before him was a far cry from the Henry who thought escaping the bad guys was a jovial game that involved costumes and one-liners. This man was scared, desperate. And most definitely not telling him the whole story.

"To bring you fucking flowers and chocolate and a lipstick print card that says 'Thanks for last night'? I don't know; what does it matter? You weren't there and Bixler already had the warrant. Val said I should take you somewhere safe."

"Val?"

"Yes, Val. Tall, black hair—"

"Henry, shut up!"

"Why are you telling me to shut up when I'm the one with the fucking information?" Henry shouted back.

"Because what you're telling me isn't something I can understand."

"Wrap your fucking shiny head around it, Mac. They're coming for you. Right now. You can either get in Penny's car and go with me, or—"

Mac knew a moment of absolute dread. "Penny's car?"

"Oh, for Christ's sake, I didn't steal it! She lent it to me. She and Val want us to run. That's the truth, and the only question right now is whether you trust me."

The look Henry gave him was pleading.

He wants *me to trust him.*

"I can't run," Mac said firmly. "That would make me look guilty."

"You *already* look guilty, Mac! The cocaine in your desk really did a number on your halo."

"I'm not guilty, and once the—"

"It doesn't *matter* if you're guilty or not! You've been set up. And for all you know, whoever's doing it has more than a bag of coke up their sleeve. You think you're gonna prove your innocence from a prison cell?"

"And what do I prove by running? That I've got something to hide."

"Val said you have to come with me. And she's your boss."

Under other circumstances, he would have laughed. But Henry was serious, fists clenched, jaw set.

"She *trusts* me," Henry added.

Mac took his phone from his pocket. "Let me call Val."

"There's no time!" Henry actually grabbed his sleeve, and when Mac met his gaze, Henry shook his arm. "At least come with me for a little while. Don't let them arrest you right now. You can come back later if you're that fucking desperate to go to jail, but for now, just— just come with me." The hitch in Henry's voice was slight, but it did more than his words could. Mac searched Henry's face for any sign of artifice. Not that there would be any. Henry was a master liar.

He opened his mouth to answer, not really sure what would come out, but then Henry went on, his speech quick and stilted: "If you go to prison I won't ever see you again."

"What do you mean?"

"I mean if you're not around, I'll run."

"No," Mac warned. "You're staying to testify."

"I'm staying for *you*!" Henry's clenched jaw trembled. "If I try a—another way of living, it's gonna be with you or not at all. I can disappear anytime I want. Any fucking time. But you make me—" He drew a quavering breath, no longer looking at Mac. "I *promised* you."

Mac didn't move. Henry's hand slid from his arm.

Logic told Mac he couldn't believe a thing this guy said, ever. But some part of him thought he was getting better at telling what was real with Henry.

Henry was trying.

Trying to learn the difference between doing the wrong thing for the wrong reasons, and doing the wrong thing because it was the only way to keep someone safe.

He was trying to help Mac. And that Scooby-Doo episode had been him trying to help his sister.

Mac wondered that he ever could have thought Henry was selfish. Foolish, yes. Dangerously so.

But never selfish.

"Okay," he said.

Henry looked up and smiled, and for a second, Mac thought he had been played after all. But the muscles in Henry's jaw and neck were still tight, and he didn't look smug, just relieved. "Then grab your fucking head polish and your toothbrush and let's go. Vi's at the hotel. I have to stop and get her."

"I didn't say I'm going with you for good. Just until I can get ahold of Val and figure this out."

"I just hope you know somewhere we can hide for a while. I don't exactly have a lot of friends now that I've stopped using the FBI recruiting poster for target practice."

"Aw, Henry." He followed Henry out the door and toward the car. "That's kind of sweet."

Henry glanced over his shoulder. "I am kind of sweet, Mac. Once you get to know me."

"You're certainly something, all right."

"Just say it. Say I'm sweet."

"You're sweet." He got into the car alongside Henry.

"Then I'm not good for you." Henry started the engine.

Mac wasn't sure what to say to that. Henry wasn't smiling.

"Your doctor," Henry continued, "said to lay off the—"

"I don't care what my doctor said."

Henry glanced at him. "You'll care someday when your heart explodes."

He backed out of the drive and floored it down the road.

It was only a short drive to the hotel. Mac's cell rang twice, and he checked in case it was Val. But both times it was a number he didn't recognize—though he could guess who it belonged to. Val wouldn't be stupid enough to call, now that he was on the lam. Now that—and Mac still wasn't sure he'd got this right—she'd organized for Henry to *take* him on the lam.

He took the battery out of his phone. Screw that. If he was being set up, and he was obviously being set up, then Henry was right—he needed to hole up somewhere long enough to think, and to figure out what the hell was going on. Why Val thought Henry should be there with him, he wasn't sure.

Because that had gone so well last time, hadn't it? If he'd learned anything when he was squirreled away with Henry in Altona, it was that he tended to do all his thinking with the wrong head.

He swore under his breath.

Henry glanced at him sharply as they entered the lobby of the hotel.

Mac pulled up short. "Anything you want to tell me, Henry? Are you involved in this mess somehow, because you've been looking at me strangely since my place. You look like a dog that stole the last sausage and is trying real hard to act like nothing happened."

"Nothing happened." Henry's tone was light, but his gaze wouldn't fix on Mac's. Slid right over him like he wasn't there. "There was no sausage and I was out back the whole time digging holes in the garden."

Mac frowned at him. "Did you know Jimmy Rasnick?"

An almost imperceptible twitch in Henry's jaw, but no answer.

"Because whoever killed Lonny Harris did it the exact same way that Rasnick shot his victims."

"Lonny's *dead*?" Henry blanched. "Shit."

Mac rubbed his aching chest. "You knew him?" he demanded.

"He was a piece of shit." Henry shook his head.

"Did you know Jimmy Rasnick?" Mac asked him.

"Everyone knows who Jimmy Rasnick was," Henry said, lifting his chin. "My mom was a junkie, remember? Did some dealing, as well. So yeah, I met the guy. Of course I met the guy."

"You told me once you didn't know Rasnick."

"Well maybe I didn't want to take a trip down memory lane then, okay?" Henry punched the call button for the elevator. "Maybe I didn't want to tell you that when I went crying to my mom's friend Jimmy fucking Rasnick about how we didn't have the money to pay for Vi's hospital, he was the one who told me I could always suck dick for a living."

"Is that true?"

"Yep."

"Is it the entire truth?" Mac was sure the flicker in Henry's eyes meant it wasn't. "Henry, I need to know this shit, okay? Because at the moment I don't know what the fuck is going on. Someone who knew Rasnick has got a hard-on for revenge, so, yeah . . ." He followed Henry into the elevator. "So I know why I'm being set up, but I'd sure as fuck like to know who's doing it."

Henry watched the numbers climb higher. "I don't know, Mac, really I don't."

"I don't believe that. This is *you*, Henry. There's always something!"

"Yeah? Fuck you." There was no anger in Henry's tone. He jiggled his leg as the elevator climbed.

Mac didn't know whether to feel guilty or vindicated. He never knew with Henry.

The elevator pinged open.

Henry led the way down the hall.

"Viola?" Henry called as he swiped his keycard and pushed the door inward. "Vi?"

Mac saw it first: a thin trail of blood across the carpet. He elbowed Henry aside, and reached for his firearm.

Henry was livid. "What are you—" His gaze dropped to the carpet. "*Viola!*"

Mac had never seen him look so suddenly, horribly afraid. Not with Dreama Carey Coleman standing over him with a syringe. Not even in the cabin in Altona.

"Stay here," he said, edging toward the bedroom door. He opened it cautiously. The room was empty. He crossed the carpet—more blood—and slid the bathroom door open.

Viola was sitting on the floor. She was holding a book open in her lap, the pages smeared with blood. She lifted her face. She was crying.

"Viola," Mac said. She looked so much like Henry that his throat ached. "Remember me?"

"I hurt my hand, Mac." Tears slid down her face.

"It's okay." He reholstered his firearm. Grabbed the washcloth off the rail and knelt down beside her on the tiles. "Let me have a look at it."

"I don't like blood," she whispered.

"Me neither," Mac said. "Henry! She's okay!"

Henry was right there. "What happened, Vi?" He tugged her injured hand toward him.

"I was cutting out a bird picture and I slipped," Viola said, her eyes wide. "Is it a lot of blood? I kept my eyes closed."

"If you hold on to the washcloth, it'll stop bleeding in a second." Henry laid the washcloth in her palm, over the cut, and curled her fingers closed. He held his hand around hers. "Why were you alone?"

"I don't know."

Henry dropped her hand. He stood, turned, and punched the wall. "That fucker! That useless junkie piece of shit!" He punched the wall again. Mac flinched at the force behind it. "Fuck!"

Mac looked from Viola to Henry. "You're scaring your sister. Calm down."

Henry made a strangled sound in the back of his throat. He squeezed his eyes shut and pressed his forehead against the wall. He opened his fists, his fingers straining. "Sorry." He straightened. "Vi, where's Remy?"

"He had to leave," Viola said in a small voice. "I said I could stay on my own."

Henry didn't respond.

"Okay," Mac said. "Viola, come and sit on the bed. It's more comfortable than the floor."

Henry watched narrow-eyed as Mac helped Viola to her feet. He settled her on the bed, made sure she was holding the washcloth tightly, and went and fetched her a bottle of water from the minibar. Then he returned to the bathroom, and to Henry.

"Want to tell me what happened here?" he asked in a low voice.

"He was supposed to be watching her." Henry's voice cracked. "He *promised* he would, but what the hell's a promise mean to an addict, right?"

Mac put a hand on Henry's shoulder. Leaned in close. "She's okay."

"Not just her, Mac! Remy was supposed to be here for you too."

"Remy?" Mac knew the name . . . or at least he'd heard or maybe read it recently. It was unusual enough to catch in his memory.

"This morning Remy told me that Lonny Harris had been paid to set up a federal agent," Henry said. He shrugged. "It's *you*, Mac. It's gotta be you."

Mac released him and stepped back. What was it he'd said to Henry in the elevator? *This is you, Henry. There's always something.* Well, what if that something turned out to be that Henry didn't just know Lonny Harris, he also knew that Harris had been paid to lie about Mac?

It had been a long time since Mac had believed in coincidences. He was taking a leap of faith on this being one now. Because Henry Page played a long con, didn't he? He lied for a living. And this was the point, right here in this hotel bathroom, where Mac had to decide whether to believe him, or whether to tell him to go fuck himself.

He could walk away.

He didn't need Henry.

He didn't.

Had Henry been trying to warn him in the car? *"Then I'm not good for you."*

Fuck.

Henry had to know he'd end up lying to Mac. Breaking his promise. He was who he was.

Henry stared at him. Opened his mouth to say something, then shut it again. Swallowed. Pressed his lips together. Swallowed again. Finally got a word out: "Mac."

He felt a rush of need. Different than lust. It was just as hot, just as desperate, but it ran deeper. He reached out and cupped Henry's face in his hands. "Promise me. Promise you're not fucking lying."

"Promise," Henry whispered. He leaned in.

Mac dropped his hands. "Pack Viola's bags. Five minutes."

Don't give me time to change my mind.

"Mac," Henry murmured, frowning. "What—"

"Five minutes." Mac kept his voice steady.

"Okay," Henry said, his eyes as wide as Viola's. "Five minutes."

Vi loved road trips. Henry saw she was smiling before they even cleared downtown.

"This is a nice car," she said.

Henry checked that the GPS jammer was working. Best. Investment. Ever. Penny wouldn't report her car as stolen until she absolutely had to, but there was no point in leaving a trail of breadcrumbs for OPR to trace in a few hours, was there?

He passed the M&M's back to Viola.

She leaned forward, and her hair snagged on the hanger from which Henry's suit hung in a long black bag. "Ow," she said, untangling herself. "Why do you have a suit? Are you going to work?"

"You never know." Henry reclaimed the M&M's. "I wouldn't want to be caught anywhere without a suit. Not even in—" He glanced at Mac as they turned off East 96th and onto I-69. "Really, Mac? We're going this way? Tell me we're heading to Muncie, please. Said no one ever."

Mac didn't answer right away. "We're going to Altona."

He opened his mouth to ask Mac what the fuck he was talking about, then stopped himself. Maybe Mac had a plan. Shit, Henry wanted to trust that he did. "I should have driven." He leaned back.

"And where would we go then?" Mac asked.

Henry shrugged.

"The Court of Miracles," Viola suggested.

"Vi." Henry sighed. "The Court is a secret, remember?"

"I remember." A note of steel crept into her voice. "But Mac is our *friend*, and secrets are bad."

"Yeah, secrets are bad." He stared out the window for a moment. "You know what else is bad?"

"What?" Viola asked.

"Sequels."

"I like *The Empire Strikes Back*," Viola said.

"So do I." Henry found his glasses in his bag and put them on. One earpiece squeaked when he opened it. "But *The Empire Strikes Back* is the exception to the rule. *Grease 2*, anyone?"

Viola passed a green M&M up between the seats, and Henry took it.

Mac watched the road.

"Sequels," Henry said, "are generally crap. Which is why I'm wondering why we're going back to Altona instead of heading for Mexico right about now. Given that last time we were at the cabin, Mac, you got shot. Remember that?"

"We're not going to the cabin," Mac said.

"Where are we going?" Henry asked.

Mac drummed his fingers on the steering wheel. "Well, I can't believe I'm actually saying this, but, Henry, I'm taking you home to meet my parents."

Henry's mouth dropped open.

Well, fuck.

That was the worst idea he'd heard in a while.

Explore the rest of the *Playing the Fool* series:
riptidepublishing.com/titles/series/playing-the-fool

Dear Reader,

Thank you for reading Lisa Henry and J.A. Rock's *The Merchant of Death*!

We know your time is precious and you have many, many entertainment options, so it means a lot that you've chosen to spend your time reading. We really hope you enjoyed it.

We'd be honored if you'd consider posting a review—good or bad—on sites like **Amazon, Barnes & Noble, Kobo, Goodreads, Twitter, Facebook, Tumblr**, and your blog or website. We'd also be honored if you told your friends and family about this book. Word of mouth is a book's lifeblood!

For more information on upcoming releases, author interviews, blog tours, contests, giveaways, and more, please sign up for our weekly, spam-free newsletter and visit us around the web:

Newsletter: tinyurl.com/RiptideSignup
Twitter: twitter.com/RiptideBooks
Facebook: facebook.com/RiptidePublishing
Goodreads: tinyurl.com/RiptideOnGoodreads
Tumblr: riptidepublishing.tumblr.com

Thank you so much for Reading the Rainbow!

RiptidePublishing.com

ALSO BY LISA HENRY

King of Dublin, with Heidi Belleau
He Is Worthy
Bliss, with Heidi Belleau
Sweetwater
Tribute
The Island
Dark Space

ALSO BY J.A. ROCK

By His Rules
Wacky Wednesday (Wacky Wednesday #1)
The Brat-tastic Jayk Parker (Wacky Wednesday #2)
Calling the Show
Take the Long Way Home (coming soon)

ALSO BY HENRY & ROCK

The Two Gentlemen of Altona (Playing the Fool #1)
When All the World Sleeps
The Good Boy (The Boy #1)
The Naughty Boy (The Boy #1.5)
The Boy Who Belonged (The Boy #2)
Mark Cooper Versus America (Prescott College #1)
Brandon Mills Versus the V-Card (Prescott College #2) (coming soon)
Another Man's Treasure

ABOUT THE AUTHORS

LISA HENRY likes to tell stories, mostly with hot guys and happily ever afters. Lisa lives in tropical North Queensland, Australia. She doesn't know why, because she hates the heat, but she suspects she's too lazy to move. She spends half her time slaving away as a government minion, and the other half plotting her escape. She attended university at sixteen, not because she was a child prodigy or anything, but because of a mix-up between international school systems early in life. She studied history and English, neither of them very thoroughly. She shares her house with too many cats, a dog, a green tree frog that swims in the toilet, and as many possums as can break in every night. This is not how she imagined life as a grown-up.

Website: lisahenryonline.com
Blog: lisahenryonline.blogspot.com.au
Twitter: twitter.com/LisaHenryOnline
Facebook: facebook.com/lisa.henry.1441

J.A. ROCK has worked as a dog groomer, knife seller, haunted house zombie, standardized patient, census taker, state fair quilt hanger, and, for one less-than-magical evening, a server—and would much rather be writing about those jobs than doing them. J.A. currently lives in Chicago but still sees West Virginia behind Illinois's back.

Website: www.jarockauthor.com
Blog: jarockauthor.blogspot.com
Twitter: twitter.com/jarockauthor
Facebook: facebook.com/ja.rock.39

Enjoy this book?
Find more romantic suspense at RiptidePublishing.com!

Running Wild
ISBN: 978-1-62649-154-0

Cross & Crown
ISBN: 978-1-62649-132-8

Earn Bonus Bucks!

Earn 1 Bonus Buck for each dollar you spend. Find out how at RiptidePublishing.com/news/bonus-bucks.

Win Free Ebooks for a Year!

Pre-order coming soon titles directly through our site and you'll receive one entry into a drawing to win free books for a year! Get the details at RiptidePublishing.com/contests.

Made in the USA
Charleston, SC
18 September 2015